TEMPERANCE

TEMPERANCE TRILOGY BOOK I

MATT PRESCOTT

The lyrics from "Roll On Silver Moon," by Charles N. Ernest.
Traditional

The lyrics from "Wait for the Wagon," by R. Bishop Buckley.
Traditional

The lyrics from "Darling Nelly Gray," by Benjamin Hanby.
Traditional

*To Linda and Emily for always going along with
my harebrained schemes,*

*My parents for inspiration
and for helping bring this to life,*

*And my Grandfather, John Oliver Kildow -
the coolest man I know*

TEMPERANCE

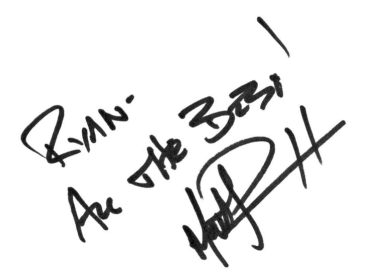

PROLOGUE

THE NIGHT Joe Dunn and his four ranch hands were gunned down in the Deadeye Saloon, Henry McCann was working behind the bar. He'd been in a piss-poor mood for most of the day and was currently taking his frustrations out on the long mahogany bar's cracked finish. As he scrubbed at a particularly stubborn stain with his frayed and yellowed wash rag, Henry couldn't help but focus on how much he hated his life.

His mood began to take its downward swing that morning as he emptied three overfull brass spittoons behind the saloon. While upending the final tarnished container, Henry slipped on the overflow, pouring rancid tobacco water down the front of his trousers. A high-pitched yelp escaped his lips as he landed on his ass in the large puddle he'd created. Catching his breath, Henry could feel the lukewarm filth seeping through the fabric and coating him from the waist down.

After a long moment he pulled himself up, wiped off as much of the liquid as he could with his bare hands and walked back into the Deadeye.

Placing the now empty spittoons where they belonged next to the bar, Henry looked around to see if any customers had arrived in his absence. Sitting at the table closest to the bar, gazing through the batwings towards the street was a young boy.

"What are you doing here, kid? You shouldn't be in a place like this."

The boy just looked at him. He was thin and slight and couldn't be more than ten years old. He had a puff of blonde hair and was wearing clothes that looked like hand-me-downs from a much larger child. He didn't say a word.

As Henry opened his mouth to question the boy, Edith Monroe, the Deadeye's only whore, came slinking out from the back room. She was a large gal, probably late thirties and rather worn looking. It was obvious she wore no undergarments under her loose, flower dress. Her dark hair was sloppily pulled up onto the top of her head.

"Don't you be givin' this child no hard time, Henry. This here's Daniel. He and his pa rode in this morning with them other cowboys and he has nowhere to go. I told him he could stay here as long as he needed while his pa gets done whatever it is he needs to get done."

"I wasn't giving him a hard time. I just—"

"Would you like some biscuits, sweetie?" she said to Daniel, cutting Henry off. "I make a mean plate of biscuits and gravy."

Daniel looked up at her and nodded slightly.

"Well, of course you do, child. I'll go whip some up."

Edith turned and slipped back into the kitchen.

"Well, kid, I guess you sitting there won't hurt anything for now. You and your pa staying somewhere in town?"

"Don't rightly know, sir." Daniel's voice was just a whisper.

"That's fine, just make sure you keep out of sight as soon as customers start showing up."

Daniel nodded and went back to looking out the door towards the street.

After a while, Edith came with a plate of biscuits smothered in sausage gravy. The smell of butter and spiced meat filled the room and woke up Henry's empty stomach. The boy made the biscuits disappear like they'd never been there.

Edith sat with Daniel for the next few hours, telling him stories and singing him songs. She had a lovely singing voice. Henry thought she'd make a much better singer than a whore.

Around six o'clock, the Deadeye saloon was full of drunk cowboys playing cards and shooting off their mouths. It wasn't a big place and it filled up quick. Edith had moved the boy to a table towards the back of the room to keep him away from the debauchery that would soon follow. For the rest of the night she would be busy with almost constant customers.

In between pouring drinks and fielding insults, Henry diligently worked to forget his place in the world by polishing a yellow spot on the old mahogany. He was so focused on the stain that he almost didn't notice a chair bouncing across the sawdust covered floor.

Joe Dunn stood up so quickly from the table where he was playing cards that his chair went flying. His hand hovered over his Remington Army revolver as he backed away.

Joe and his ranch hands were regulars of the Deadeye and played cards there almost nightly. He did tend to be a loudmouth though, and it wasn't that surprising he was starting trouble.

After Joe stood, four of his men joined him, spreading out across the saloon. All of them had their hands over their revolvers.

"I knew you was cheatin' me. Get up, goddamn it," Joe spat at a man sitting on the other side of the table.

Henry couldn't make out the man's face. He was sitting in a dark corner of the room shrouded in shadow with a bottle of rye whiskey and a glass in front of him.

"I ain't gonna tell you again, you son of a bitch. Get up!" Joe yelled.

He looked to his men to make sure they were backing him up.

Billy Boone, one of Joe's younger hands stood to his left with his hands over his two revolvers. He was small and quick and way too eager to get into a fight. Behind Joe was Clive, Billy's older brother. He was taller, wore an old bowler and had thick sideburns. He carried one sidearm and was much more subtle than his little brother. Hank Chapman was older and stood next to Clive. He had a big belly, a hunched back and an old six-shooter which looked brand new despite its age. Oscar Ruiz was on Joe's right, next to the bar. He was quiet and stocky. He carried one revolver and looked like he knew how to use it.

TEMPERANCE

The man in the corner just sat there and looked back at Joe. As he reached for the bottle of rye, Joe flinched. The man paused for a second. Then poured himself a drink. He nodded to the room and downed the glass.

Henry vaguely remembered the stranger asking for a bottle of rye whiskey earlier that evening but never got a solid look at his face. Now all he could see of him was his dark shirt, dark pants and dusty brown boots. The stranger wore a flat-brimmed, dark hat.

Joe remained standing, waiting for the stranger to make a move. Henry could tell that Joe's effort to be intimidating was waning and that maybe he was in over his head.

Finally, the stranger pushed back his chair and slowly stood up. After pocketing his winnings he paused and looked at the room. Joe, Billy, Clive, Hank and Oscar stared him down, their hands hovering over their weapons. The stranger picked up the bottle of rye with his left hand and moved to the center of the saloon. Henry still couldn't see his face but he could see his low hung, ivory-handled Colt tied to his leg.

The stranger stood with the bottle in his left hand and his right thumb stuck behind his belt buckle. He looked at Joe and Joe looked back. The longer they stood there, the more nervous Joe seemed to appear. The saloon was completely quiet. Everyone other than the stranger, Joe and his ranch hands had somehow moved to the back of the room. Henry began to feel his stomach turn from the tension.

The stranger raised the bottle to his mouth and took a swig.

Joe saw his opportunity, drew his gun and pulled the trigger. A puff of sawdust exploded about three feet in front of him. Henry couldn't understand why the shot was so short until he saw blood spray from the back of Joe's head and onto Hank Chapman's face.

Henry quickly looked back to the stranger who was just finishing his bottle of rye, holding his smoking, ivory-handled Colt in his right hand at his hip.

The rest of Joe's men stood in shock and disbelief. The stranger paused for a second then dropped the empty bottle and fanned the rest of his rounds into Billy, Clive, Hank and Oscar before the bottle hit the ground. It bounced and spun in a circle at his feet.

The room was full of smoke and the smell of spent gunpowder as Henry stood frozen behind the bar, holding his wash cloth, trying to comprehend what he'd just seen.

The stranger calmly reloaded his Colt, spun it and slid it back into its holster. He bent over and picked up the empty bottle of rye.

Henry looked at the stranger as he approached the bar but in his shock, still couldn't make out his face. The stranger set the empty bottle on the old mahogany with his gun hand and stood for a moment facing the batwings.

Just below the stranger's rolled up sleeve on his right forearm was a brand in the shape of a heart. It wasn't a random scar, it was definitely a brand.

As the stranger turned towards the door, a scream came from the back of the room.

"He shot him! He shot the boy!" From the far corner, Edith Monroe cradled a small body in her arms and sobbed. "He shot the boy."

In the darkness, Henry could just make out the blonde puff of hair of the boy who had come into the saloon earlier that day. His body was limp and bloody. There was no sign of life.

As Henry struggled to breathe, he looked towards the stranger who had stopped mid-stride. The stranger hesitated for a moment then slowly made way for the rusty batwings that made a melancholy howl as he slipped through them.

Henry McCann fell backwards against the wall and began to cry.

ONE

BECKETT WAS BENT OVER a cold mountain stream when he heard the first gruesome howl come through the trees. When he heard the second, he dropped his tarnished metal pan on the gravel of the bank and stood alert. The third ghostly cry confirmed his suspicions.

He grabbed his worn, leather saddlebag, left his pan on the bank, knowing full well that there would be no gold in it, and mounted his sorrel. After climbing through the thick ponderosa pines and up the rocky slope back out of the ravine, Beckett kicked his horse to a gallop and headed to the clearing where he'd set the trap.

Just before the tree line ended, he slid out of the saddle, tossed his hat aside and threw a loop of rope over his shoulder. The now chest-rumbling howl echoed through the trees as he tied his sorrel to a low limb.

Beckett pulled his large Bowie knife from a holster-like sheath that was tied to his right thigh. He wore it low like a gunfighter would wear a Colt. Its elk-horn handle was well polished from years of use and felt at home in his large hand. It had a huge, fourteen-inch blade that was heavy but perfectly balanced and razor sharp. The knife might have looked like a small sword in some people's hands but at over six feet tall and with a body of almost solid muscle, it just made Beckett look deadly.

As he eased into the dry, pine-needle-covered clearing, he finally saw his opponent face-to-face.

A large black bear stood just a couple of yards in front of him. Its dark black shoulders rose three feet from the ground and its open, panting mouth showed huge yellow teeth. Beckett could see both terror and anger in the animal's glossy, black eyes.

The bear didn't come any closer because it was caught in a large bear trap he had set two days earlier. It seemed to be holding the animal securely enough despite one major problem - instead of catching the bear on one of its front paws as Beckett had planned, the trap was tightly clamped on the bear's left hind paw. The animal must have backed into the trap while smelling the over-ripe bait. Now, the dangerous part of the animal was free to thrash, lunge and bite while only being pinned from behind.

Beckett holstered his Bowie, grabbed the rope from his shoulder and tied a makeshift lasso out of it. It wasn't the perfect rope for the task - the ones he'd used on cattle were much stiffer - but it would have to do. Beckett slowly stepped closer, paused a moment then tossed the lasso around the bear's neck. He quickly cinched it tight and pulled against the animal. The bear reared up on its remaining hind leg. Raised at full length, it towered over seven feet. Beckett was no match for its strength so he found a nearby tree and tied the rope around it.

He ran out of the clearing to his grazing sorrel, jumped on and slowly rode towards the struggling black bear. When the horse saw the angered, trapped animal it hesitated and began to back up. Beckett leaned over and calmed the horse, stroking its mane and willing it to move forward.

Once he reached the rope, he untied it and attached it to the saddle horn. He then led his sorrel away from the bear and around a tree. The strength of the horse pulled the bear tight between the tree and the trap, hanging it by its neck horizontally.

As the bear struggled against the tightening rope, Becket slowly approached it. He carefully unsheathed his Bowie and stood just out of striking distance of the bear's thrashing claws.

He positioned himself at the back end of the struggling animal, took a couple of quick steps and jumped on top, straddling it. Leaning forward, he placed his large hand on the bear's brow and drew the fourteen-inch Bowie across its neck.

Even though the blade was razor sharp, it took several strong strokes to cut all the way to the bone. In the interim, the bear was able to swipe backwards one last time, catching Beckett on the arm, gouging flesh and almost tearing off his sleeve.

As the bear's blood began to pour out, its strength waned. While holding on to the animal's back, Beckett whispered condolences into the bear's ear, thanking it for its sacrifice. Finally, the huge animal slumped to the hard earth, its life drained. With no more resistance from the rope, his horse eased up and resumed grazing on sparse greens as if nothing had happened.

Beckett fell against the still warm fur of the bear, drained from his exertion and rush of adrenaline. He could smell the thick musk of the animal and the iron from the pool of blood forming beneath. Beckett eventually pulled himself off, limped over to a small boulder in the middle of the clearing and collapsed against it.

For a moment, he enjoyed the warmth of the morning sun rising in the sky. A warm breeze brought the smell of sap and pine needles and the distant hum of summer cicadas. The peaceful scene was immediately destroyed by the screaming pain in his arm. Before long he was unable to focus on anything but his agony.

His shirt was torn at the shoulder seam and his long underwear was tattered. There were a couple of deep punctures on his shoulder and one long gash across his upper arm. He stiffly heaved himself up and limped over to his grazing sorrel.

"Thanks for the help, buddy."

The horse snorted and ignored him.

He untied his saddlebag then pulled a small leather purse from a storage pocket at the back of the saddle. He dragged himself back to the boulder and slumped down.

Withdrawing a small bottle of whiskey from the saddlebag, he popped the cork with his teeth and took a swig. The liquid burned all the way down his throat, warming his stomach and producing instant calm. He dug through the bag for a tied up ball of clean rags made from boiled strips of an old bed sheet.

Gritting his teeth, he doused the wound with a few shots of whiskey and began to clean the clotting blood from his shoulder and arm. He then opened the small leather purse and removed a needle and four types of thread.

"What color do you think would look best: black, red, green, or blue?"

His sorrel was oblivious to anything but his grazing.

"Yup, blue would match my eyes. Good choice."

Beckett tore a length of blue thread, tied it off, fed it through the needle, then dipped everything into the whiskey bottle.

It took six stitches to completely close the wound after which he doused the area with more whiskey. When he was finished he covered the makeshift surgery with another fabric strip, closed his eyes and passed out.

* * *

An hour after cleaning, gutting and building a sled to transport the bear, Beckett arrived at his cabin. The structure was small but sturdy, made of pine logs stacked one on another. The front wall was about two feet taller than the rear, allowing the roof to angle back so that drainage went away from the entrance. Alongside the cabin was an old stable in dire need of repair and next to it was a small smokehouse. He would eventually hang the butchered parts of the bear here but first, he and his horse needed rest.

TEMPERANCE

After unloading his gear and attending to his horse, he stumbled through the front door and collapsed onto a lumpy, hay-filled mattress.

TWO

TWO YEARS EARLIER, Beckett stepped off of a fancy new locomotive in a town called Rathdrum. He wore a huge buffalo-skin coat that still smelled of the animal. His boots were old and worn but his pants and shirt were brand new, bought the day before from a shop in Missoula. The clothes he'd been wearing at the time had the look and smell of having been worn the last six months while he'd hunted and skinned buffalo. The change of attire was something he was sure his fellow passengers appreciated.

Rathdrum was a large town full of criss-crossing dirt streets. It was nowhere near the size of San Francisco or Chicago but for the Idaho Territory panhandle, it was big. The sidewalks were made of wood planks and most of the brick buildings were fitted with cloth awnings. At midday, the dusty streets were bustling, full of carts, horses and people.

Beckett stepped up onto one of the wooden sidewalks and strolled the main street, his saddle over his shoulder. As an older woman wearing a large feathered hat nodded to him, he tipped his hat to her in passing.

A few blocks later he came upon a rundown saloon called Shotgun Willie's. He placed his saddle on the hitching post out front between a sorrel and a small paint, removed his saddlebag and walked through the open front door.

Shotgun Willie's was a large place with poker and faro to the right and stairs to "billiards" towards the back. The bar was long and polished and manned by a single bartender. At the far end of the bar in the corner were two stools that faced the door. One of the stools was empty. On the other sat an old man.

Beckett squeezed in next to the old man and placed his saddlebag on the bar. The bartender sauntered over to him, spitting on the lenses of his wire frame glasses then cleaning them with his apron.

"What'll it be?" The bartender held his glasses up to the light, checking for any additional smudges.

"What kinda beer you got back there?"

"Got the kind that comes in a bottle."

"That'll do."

The bartender placed his glasses back on his face, reached below the bar and pulled out a tall, brown bottle. He popped the latched seal and slid it in front of Beckett who took a swig. The beer was warm, flat and watered down.

"Thought fer a second a bear was 'bout to attack me," the old man next to him said. "Where'd the hell you get a coat like that?"

"From a buffalo."

The old man looked him up and down. "Get it with your bare hands, did ya? Don't see no gun."

"Used a knife."

"You mean that gutter you got on yer thigh?" The old man gestured to Beckett's holstered Bowie.

"That's the one."

"You tellin' me you killed a Buffalo with just that knife?"

"Yup."

"Why didn't you use a rifle like a civilized feller?"

"Well, that wouldn't have been as much fun now would it?"

The old man let out a loud belly laugh, pounded a shot of whiskey, slapped the bar and signaled for another.

"Ye ha! I like you, boy. Name's Oliver Crow. I'd be glad to know yours if'n you'd oblige me."

The old man was small, probably in his late seventies. He wore a ratty old hat and a vest made of what appeared to be beaver. He was white, but his skin was red and leathery like an Indian. A long white beard framed his pock-marked face. Beckett instantly liked him.

"You can call me Beckett."

"Well, Mr. Beckett, can you tell me why, in this here empty bar, you gone and took the seat right next to me?"

"Like to keep an eye on the room. You know, just in case this buffalo's cousin has it in for me and comes blazin' through the front door."

"So'n you can kill it with your knife there?" Oliver said, chuckling.

"Somethin' like that."

"Well, if'n you want a view of this here room, that poker table in the corner looks 'bout the best spot. How 'bout losin' a few hands to an ornery old man?"

"Be happy to."

Oliver grabbed the old Sharps rifle he had leaning next to the bar and used it as a cane. He took a seat at the table across the room and Beckett followed.

As the two played cards in the dark saloon, more words were exchanged than money.

"I don't get a chance to talk with folks much no more, livin' up in them mountains an all." Oliver held his cards loosely and let them drop forward as he talked.

Beckett tried not to look out of courtesy, but most of the time it was impossible to miss Oliver's hand. He let the old man win from time to time to keep the game going.

Having given up on the beer, Beckett now shared a bottle of whiskey with his partner at the table. As Beckett filled both their glasses, Oliver pulled out an old corn cob pipe and lit it.

"What's an old timer like you doin' up in those mountains anyway? I thought these parts were trapped out decades ago."

"Do a little trappin', still a few beaver left up there. Pelts ain't worth much no more though. Kinda' like it up there all alone. It's peaceful. Well, it was until last summer."

Oliver downed his shot of whiskey and took a couple of puffs from his pipe. Beckett drained his as well and refilled their glasses again.

"What happened last summer?"

"Now, I ain't quite up on current events, being up in'em mountains and all, but I guess sometime a few years ago, some fellers started findin' gold in the rock 'round here. Well, now, I bet you can guess what happened next."

"People start comin' up here in droves?"

"Damn right that's what happened." The old man slapped the table making the few coins on it jingle. "Stick a pickaxe in a mountain and find gold and the vultures swarm. Even built a railroad so they could get them fancy new steam engines up here to haul in more folks. I heard Fort Sherman's got steam ships down on Coeur d'Alene Lake hauling rocks and men from the mines on the river."

"I heard that too."

"That why you come up here? For the gold and what-not?"

"Nope. Was headin' to Seattle to meet a friend who said he had some work for me. Got tired of the train so I decided to get off here. I'll probably head that way again."

"That's good. Glad you ain't one of 'em greedy bastards."

"Well, I can tell you I ain't greedy. Can't tell you I ain't a bastard though."

Oliver let out another loud belly laugh and almost fell backwards out of his seat.

"Beckett, you's a real card, you know that?"

"So, have the miners been givin' you a hard time up at your place?"

"Well, I guess it ain't really been all that bad. After all this gold business started, fellers started dividing up the mountains into things they call claims. Guess you claim it's

20

yours and it's yours. Well, seein' that I've been up in my cabin goin' on forty years now, and the fact that I'm an ornery son of a bitch, they figured it was easier to just to call my land and the stream that goes through it a gold claim. Even gave me a fancy, signed piece of paper provin' it."

"There any gold on your gold claim?"

"Hell if I know. Got me one of 'em siftin' pans for the stream but I can't find nothin'. Didn't move up there for gold anyway, moved up there to get away from the assholes down here in the towns."

"I have to tell you I'm kinda envious of your place up there in the mountains." Beckett took another shot of whiskey. "Get tired of dealin' with folks in towns. Always someone lookin' to shoot you in the back."

"Well ya ain't gonna get away from that in Seattle."

"Probably not," Beckett said, sitting back in his chair. "How much a claim like yours go for you think?"

"Don't rightly know. Didn't pay nothin' for mine. Don't really care too much 'bout money.

"Maybe I ought to forgo Seattle and try and get me one of them claims. Think those mountains might do me some good."

"Tell you what, Mister Beckett. If you like the idea of my life up in 'em mountains so much, how 'bout I give you a chance to win my claim from me?"

"Win it?"

"That's right. You deal the cards and if your hand beats mine, you get my land."

"And what do you get if I lose?"

"How 'bout that fancy coat of yers? Always wanted me a buffalo-skin coat."

"That don't seem quite fair. Your land is worth a lot more than my coat."

"Bullshit it ain't. Just told you I don't care 'bout money. There's streams and land and cabins all over these here mountains. There ain't a lot of buffalo-skin coats though.

"Alright, you got a deal."

Beckett shuffled and dealt five cards apiece. He poured more whiskey for both of them then picked up his cards. Queen, deuce, three, six and another queen.

"Sure you want to do this?" Beckett said.

"Sure do."

Oliver picked up his cards and downed his shot glass. Beckett couldn't help but see two aces in his flailing hand.

"Well, son. What'cha got?"

Beckett laid down his cards. "Pair of Queens, looks like."

Oliver looked down at Beckett's cards and took another big puff on his pipe. Then he slammed his cards face down onto the table.

"Son, it's your lucky day. Your Queens beat what I got."

"Are you sure? Did you even look at your cards?"

"I looked at 'em and you beat me fair and square."

"Oliver, I can't take your land."

"The hell you can't. I made this bet and you won. The land is yours. Besides, I came into town today to sell that damn gold claim. Tired of all the assholes 'round here ... not includin' you, of course. This just saves me the trouble of haggling a price with some back stabber."

Beckett sat with his mouth open for a full five seconds trying to figure out what to say.

"How bout you put some whiskey in that jaw before a fly hops in it?" Oliver said, smiling.

"I have to give you something for the land. I wouldn't feel right just taking it. I have a pouch of coins. I could—"

"Told you I don't care 'bout money. Didn't pay for the damn thing anyway," Oliver said, cutting Beckett off. "But, if you really feel that bad about it, I'm sure we can work out some sorta deal."

The two men made their way out of Shotgun Willie's into the October sun. Beckett's saddlebag was back over his shoulder while Oliver Crow wore his newly acquired buffalo fur coat, limping onto the wooden sidewalk on his Sharps cane.

"Gonna have to stop by the livery so I can pick me up a horse," Beckett said. "Sold mine back in Montana for a train ticket."

"The hell you do. This here sorrel comes with the deal," Oliver said gesturing towards one of the horses out front. "I ain't got no use for two horses no more and I've had this old paint for too long to give her up."

Beckett raised his hand to object but Oliver cut him off.

"And don't even start in on how this deal ain't fair to me. I got's me a fancy coat and some freedom. I'm as happy as an old coot can get."

"Well thank you Oliver. He's a beautiful animal."

"Bullshit he is. He's old and ornery like me. You'll be doin' me a favor takin' him off my hands."

Oliver hobbled up onto his small paint, loudly refusing any help while Beckett saddled his sorrel. It had a shiny chestnut coat and a chocolate mane.

Once they were both packed up and ready they made their way down the dusty streets of Rathdrum and east into the mountains to Beckett's new gold claim.

"One other thing you could do for me if'n you're still feelin' guilty bout our deal," Oliver said.

"Anything."

"Tell me how you killed a buffalo with just a big knife."

"Well now, that's some story," Beckett said with as much drama as he could muster. "First I rode along side of it, carefully judging my distance, herding it in the direction I wanted it to go. Then, once I had it in just the right position ... the Indians I was with impaled it with arrows and spears until it collapsed."

"Injuns?"

"Yup, and once it was down I pulled my Bowie, bent over it and slit its throat. That pretty much killed it."

Oliver laughed so hard he almost fell out of his saddle.

"Beckett, you really is somethin' else."

THREE

BECKETT WOKE with a start as the sun began to peek through the trees and into his cabin. He sat straight up, catching his breath then wiping the dampness from his forehead with a trembling hand. After calming himself, he spun his legs onto the dirty wood floor and raised his arm to stretch the stiffness out of his sore right shoulder. It had been three weeks since his encounter with the black bear. His wounds had healed but were still tender.

The cabin was compact but comfortable. The walls were made of stacked logs and clay filler and were covered with various hooks for hanging clothing, tools and gear. There were no pictures or decorations.

To the left of the bed was the door and a small window of warped glass that distorted the images outside. Directly across from the bed was a stone fireplace circled by blackened river rock. To the right of the bed was a small table with an oil-powered lantern centered on it. Next to the lantern were a pen and inkwell sitting atop a wooden box with a flip-top lid.

Beckett eased himself up, moved to the old table, sat down and placed the inkwell and pen in front of him. After pulling out a folded piece of paper from the small box and lighting the lantern he began to write. The movements of his pen were slow and deliberate. He wrote steadily without stopping until the page was full then sat back, staring at the flickering filament of the oil lamp.

Once the ink was dry, Beckett folded the piece of paper, reached for his saddlebag and pulled out a plain, brown envelope. Inside were many other folded pieces of paper, forcing him to work at wedging in the new one. Once he did so, he carefully replaced the envelope back inside the saddlebag and laid it on the bed before standing and stretching.

After dressing, he pulled a large, teardrop-shaped leather bag from one of the hooks and filled it with his writing utensils, some dried meat and other supplies. He then grabbed his lantern and stepped outside.

The warmth of the late summer morning hit him like a soft blanket. He had on the same red flannel shirt he'd worn when the bear thrashed him, the arm sloppily sewn back on at the shoulder seam. His sleeves were rolled up to the elbows, revealing yellowed and dirty long underwear. He wore pants of a thick tan fabric that matched the dusty color of his flat-brimmed hat. When he moved into the cabin two years ago, his beard was close cropped. Now it was very long and ratty around the mouth. Hints of grey were sneaking into the shaggy brown hair above his ears and around his tanned, leathery jaw.

Both his sorrel and a small brown pack mule were tied to a hitch inside the stable next to his cabin. Beckett saddled his horse and attached a leather mount to the back of the pack mule. He led both animals out of the stable and tied them to a tree.

After securing the cured bear hide, a few beaver pelts and his forty-pound bear trap to the back of the mule, he grabbed the teardrop-shaped bag and mounted his sorrel.

Instead of heading the seventy miles west to Rathdrum, Beckett rode southeast towards the Coeur d'Alene river and a town called Temperance. Since the discovery of gold, mining towns had suddenly popped up all along the river, each just as wild, lawless and dangerous as the next. Temperance was no different despite its name. Becket made the trip only a few times a year whenever he was low on supplies and had something to trade.

The mountains around the Coeur d'Alene river were dotted with small lakes and streams. Beckett stopped at one around midday and took a quick, frigid bath.

After trimming his hair and his out-of-control beard he noticed two dark eyes spying on him. Less than twenty feet to his right was what looked like a small wolf, standing motionless behind a bush. Beckett rose up slowly to get a better look at the animal. Instead of a wolf, he realized it was actually a dog, a mutt really, about the size of a coyote. It had thick, mottled grey fur except for its right front paw and the tip of its tail which were white. Its ears stood erect and alert. Beckett knelt down again to make himself less threatening.

"Come 'ere boy."

The mutt just stood there and looked back at him. Beckett slowly moved over to his saddlebag and retrieved a small piece of jerky. He knelt down again.

"Come 'ere boy," he held out the jerky. "Hungry?"

Beckett took a couple of small steps closer to the mutt but it backed away. He paused for a second then tossed the piece of meat toward the animal. The mutt paused for a moment then snatched the meat from the rocks and disappeared into the pines.

"You're welcome," Beckett yelled after it.

After dressing in his clean but damp clothes, Beckett climbed onto his horse and guided it and his mule back down the mountain.

Just outside of Temperance, as the thick pines gave way to cleared land, Beckett pivoted in his saddle. Trailing cautiously behind was his new furry admirer.

FOUR

"THE DAMN fool's gonna get himself killed if he keeps it up is all I'm sayin'," Jasper Baines said as he moved a broom randomly across the wooden floor of his general store.

"Well, at least someone around here's man enough to stand up to those bullies."

"You want I should go out there and risk my neck and lose everything we got to prove I'm a man?"

"That's not what I meant, Jasper. Wasn't talking about you. You know that," Lilly said, stacking cans of peas behind the counter. "You ain't like that. Wouldn't have married you if you were."

"Well, if Byron Carter's got a beef with them boys, he'd best stay in that saloon and drink it gone. If he walks out into that street again, he's gonna prove he's a man alright. A dead man."

"Who's a dead man?" said a large figure standing in the open doorway of the store.

BECKETT ENTERED the overstocked yet tidy shop with his saddlebag over his shoulder. He'd kicked dust off his boots on the sidewalk outside because the floor inside looked spotless. He wished he'd done a better job of it when he noticed the trail of dirt that followed him into the store.

"Well, I'll be. Look who it is, Lilly." Jasper leaned his broom against a shelf full of dry goods and headed toward the door.

"Mister Beckett!" Lilly said. "Been a long time."

"How are you?" Jasper said, shaking Beckett's hand.

"I'm good," Beckett said. "Who's a dead man?"

"Oh, just some local fella lookin' to get himself in trouble. You know how it is in these mining towns." Jasper nervously brushed nonexistent dust from his clean white apron. "Didn't know if we were gonna ever see you again. Been such a long time we thought you might have moved on."

"Just lost track of time I guess. How you folks been?"

"We're good. Business is good. Town just keeps growin'," Jasper said.

Lilly came out from behind the counter. She was tall, thin and attractive. To strangers she seemed reserved though in reality she had a warm personality. Her orange floral dress was covered by a clean white apron like her husband's.

"Samuel talks about you all the time," she said. "He's always playing mountain man out in the trees. Caught himself a squirrel in a trap he made not too long ago. He'd love to see you if you're staying."

"It would be great to see him too," Beckett said. "I should be around for a little while. Need some supplies."

"Be happy to get you set up," Jasper said. "What do you need?"

"Oh, a few things. If I made you a list, would you be able to put it together for me to pick up in a couple of days?"

"Absolutely! Let me get you a pencil and paper." Jasper leaned down and rifled through items hidden beneath the counter. He was a little older than Lilly and about a foot shorter. He had a modest mustache and a thinning head of greased-back hair. He wore no glasses, but squinted in his search, indicating he might need them. His outfit was as immaculately clean as the store he kept.

"Here you go," he said, sliding the paper and pencil over to Beckett. "Would you like me to put it on store credit?"

"No, I'll pay for it like usual," Beckett said. "You still cash out gold pieces?"

"Sure. Can't do anything too big though. You'd have to take it to the new bank if that's the case. You strike it rich up there?"

"Not quite," Beckett said, reaching into his saddlebag. "See what you can give me for that."

He placed a very small leather pouch onto the counter before writing his list on the piece of paper.

Jasper picked up the pouch, took it over to a set of scales and emptied the contents onto one of the pans, carefully inspecting the small, shiny pile of metal. He then placed the smallest counterweight on the opposite pan, watched the gauge then placed another small weight on it.

"Well, I can definitely cover this Mister Beckett."

Beckett handed over his list. "Will it take care of what I need?"

Jasper looked over the list then fingered some math in the air above his head.

"Sure. Might even have a little left over."

"Great. I'll be back for it in a couple of days."

Beckett was about to make his goodbyes as he headed out the door when he heard a pat, pat, pat of small feet on the wood sidewalk outside. A young boy slid to a stop across the dusty entrance of the store.

"You're here!" the boy said. "I saw your sorrel out front. I knew you'd come back."

He dove at Beckett and threw his arms around his middle. Beckett smiled and hugged the boy back.

"Samuel! Leave poor Mister Beckett be," Lilly said. "He doesn't need you smothering him like that."

"Oh, it's fine," Beckett said to Lilly. Looking down at Samuel he added, "'Course I came back. Would have told you if I wasn't."

Samuel was eleven and small for his age, a trait probably inherited from his father. He had a mop of brown hair on top of his round head. Every time Beckett had seen him, he was smiling and eager to please. He wore nice clothes that his parents had ordered for him from the Sears and Roebuck catalog though they were now covered in dust.

"I got so much to tell you. I caught me a squirrel in that trap you showed me how to build."

"That's what I hear. You been catchin' any fish in that creek out back?"

"You bet I have. Caught me a rainbow about the size of my leg last month."

"Wish I could've seen that one." Beckett turned to the boy's parents. "Well, I'd better get goin'. Got some other stuff to take care of while I'm here. I'll see you in a couple of days to pick up those items."

"You're stayin' for supper, ain't you, Mr. Beckett?"

"I'm sure Mister Beckett is plenty busy, Samuel," Lilly interrupted with a hint of desperation in her voice. "He said he'd be by in a couple of days. I'm sure you'll be able to see him then."

"But I'm sure he ain't too busy for supper. You ain't busy are you, Mr. Beckett?"

"Actually, I have someplace I need to be this evening. We'll have to make it some other time, Samuel."

Samuel's shoulders dropped like the air was suddenly let out of him.

"When I come back to pick up my supplies in a few days, maybe we can throw a couple of lines into that old creek and see if we can't put that big rainbow to shame," Beckett said.

The boy brightened again. "Really? You mean it?

"Sure." Beckett tousled the boy's hair. "Until then …"

He tipped his hat to the boy's parents then turned and walked out onto the wooden sidewalk.

Temperance had almost doubled in size in the six months since he'd last been there. At that time, Jasper Baines' general store stood at the far end of town. Now it was halfway down the long street that stretched a quarter of a mile from end to end. At the far end it t-boned a cross street to the east, called Williams Street, named after Abe Williams, a miner who first made camp on the mountain creek that flowed below the town and was later shot in the back.

Flat front buildings made of raw wood lined the street. At the east end on the same side as the general store stood Sherman Saloon. Directly across the thoroughfare on the northeast corner was the Main Street Hotel. Centered directly between them on the east side of Williams was a building that used to be a shipping depot. Now a large "Sheriff" sign hung prominently above the door. To the right was a building new to Beckett with a door reading "Cain and Sons Bank."

The new sheriff's building had a view of the entire town. It had a small window out front and a large, thick door. The walls were made of stacked railroad ties, reinforced with steel beams. In front was a porch with three chairs all of which were empty. The porch was covered by a wooden awning held up by four thick posts.

A man with a star on his vest was leaning against one of the posts, looking out toward Main. He was tall and thin and wore black pants over dusty brown boots with a white shirt and a black vest. An ivory-handled Colt sat low on his right side, tied to his leg. The thumb of his right hand rested behind his belt buckle and above it was a black leather armband that reached from his wrist to just below his elbow. His eyes were hidden below his black, flat-brimmed hat but his small mouth was clearly visible, centered on his thin face. Probably the most striking thing about the man was his tie. It was thin and black but in the center of it was a pin about the size of a walnut made of silver that framed a huge, sparkling ruby. Beckett had never seen a gem that large and was mesmerized by it.

"That'd be Deputy Cincinnati. He ain't someone you want to mess with."

Beckett looked down at the voice behind him. Samuel was standing a few paces back following him like a shadow.

"Cincinnati?" Beckett said. "What kind of name's Cincinnati?"

"Don't know. That's just what they call him. I'm thinkin' he's usin' Cincinnati instead of his real name 'cause he's done somethin' bad and don't want to get caught."

"You think he's a bad man, do you?"

"Oh, I know he's a bad man. I ain't the only one who thinks so neither. Lots of folks sayin' he's Duke Valentine." Samuel paused, waiting for a response. "You know, the feller who shot and killed five men and a kid in Colorado ten years ago. Read all about it in this here dime novel."

Samuel pulled a rolled up book from his back pocket. He handed it to Beckett. The cover said "Duke Valentine's Day" in bold lettering. Below it was an illustration of a man wearing all black with a smoking gun in his hand. At his feet was a pile of bodies, limp and bloody. On the man's lower right arm was a mark in the shape of a heart.

"See that mark on his arm? That's a brand. Some say he got it by stealing cattle, others say his father gave it to him for disobeyin' him. Cincinnati wears that leather armband so's to hide it. Says it helps him draw quicker but I know the real reason."

"You ought not be readin' stuff like this. Just a bunch of nonsense."

"Oh, but it ain't. Mr. Boggs down at the livery thinks the same thing. So does Seamus McCready over at the butcher shop. Duke Valentine is a cold-blooded killer and now he's a deputy in our town."

"Cold blooded killers don't just get made deputies."

"They do if Sheriff Walter Cain is running the town. He bought up all the claims this side of the river and took over the town a few months ago. Appointed himself sheriff and made his two sons deputies. A few weeks later this Cincinnati feller showed up and Cain made him head deputy. They say Cain hired him on account of his sons are terrible with guns."

"Walter Cain runs the town?"

"Yup. Bought up all the claims and built a big mine down the river. Bought up half the town too. Turned the shipping depot into a jail and opened a bank."

"Could be he's just a business man lookin' to help the town grow."

"No way. My pa won't tell you but Walter Cain's been leaning on all the folks who live here for what he calls tax money. Got everyone livin' scared."

A loud crash made them both turn toward Williams Street. A man with a half full bottle of whiskey had fallen through the batwings of Sherman Saloon and smashed through a cart out front. He stumbled to his feet and staggered into the street.

"I ain't gonna take this shit from you or your boss no more, Cincinnati," the man said, drunkenly throwing his bottle aside.

"That's Byron Carter," Samuel said. "He had an argument with the deputy earlier today. Got kicked to the dirt for his trouble. Been in the saloon ever since."

Carter looked down and haphazardly pulled his holstered gun. He waved it in Cincinnati's general direction.

"You tell Cain I want my money back. If you don't, we're going to have a serious problem."

Cincinnati slowly eased himself away from the post he'd been leaning against and took three deliberate steps down to the dirt street.

"Mr. Carter," Cincinnati said, slowly closing the gap between them. "The only problem Sheriff Cain is going to have if you don't holster your weapon and leave immediately is a dead body to clean up."

"Are you threatening me, you son of a bitch?"

"The only threat I wish to alert you to is the one you've brought upon yourself. You are apparently under the impression that by standing in the middle of the street, pointing a loaded weapon at a sheriff's deputy, you have the upper hand. Well, I humbly beg to differ. I, Mr. Carter, am not a man you want to point a gun at." Cincinnati paused and casually placed his palm on the butt of his revolver.

Carter grasped his gun with both hands in an attempt to keep it steady on his target. His eyes darted to the people gathering on either side of the street.

Cincinnati resumed his pace. "You see, at this moment, you've already made the first move. Your weapon is unholstered and aimed, generally, at me. This is when you would typically say 'drop your weapon' or something to that effect. Actually, let's assume you observed protocol and just said 'drop your weapon'. Well now … I am not going to. Not only that, I'm slowly closing the gap between us, increasing your chance to hit me even in your inebriated state. So where's that leave you now?"

Carter's mouth opened as if to answer but no words came out.

"Well, Mr. Carter, you have two options. Your first option would be to pull the trigger and miraculously hit me in the chest or head before I can draw my weapon. This would eliminate the threat of me killing you but wouldn't solve your problem with Sheriff Cain. Now, your second option is a little bit easier …"

In a flash, Cincinnati's Colt was in his hand and smoking. The gunshot threw Byron Carter backwards into the dirt.

"… I draw and kill you faster than you can even pull a trigger." Cincinnati's small mouth spread into a wide smile. His large white teeth glittered like the jewel around his neck.

Before realizing what he was doing, Beckett was in the street with his hand on the handle of his Bowie.

"Get him, Mr. Beckett," Samuel said behind him.

Beckett caught himself before he got any further, hoping that the deputy hadn't taken notice of his advance. He paused then glanced at Cincinnati who looked back with a curious stare. Beckett turned back to the boy.

"Get back. You don't need to see this," he said, grabbing the boy by the shoulders and escorting him back to his parents' store.

"I told you he was a bad man, Beckett."

"Yeah, I'm beginning to think you're right."

"Were you gonna fight him?"

"There'd be no point in fightin' a man like that."

Cincinnati watched them leave. As he stood over Byron Carter's dead body, he replaced his spent round, his smile even wider than before.

"If someone wouldn't mind coming out here and cleaning up this mess, I'm sure the people of Temperance would greatly appreciate it."

FIVE

AFTER DELIVERING SAMUEL back to his parents at their store, Beckett made his way toward Williams Street. He walked more deliberately than before, hoping to avoid any contact with the deputy. Cincinnati had resumed his place holding up the post in front of the sheriff's office and was watching a couple of Chinamen heft Byron Carter's corpse into a wooden wheelbarrow. As Beckett reached the entrance of Sherman Saloon, he stood only a few yards across the street from the deputy. He kept his head down and his eyes straight ahead as he pushed open the batwings.

"You must be new in town." Cincinnati's voice cut across the dusty street, causing Beckett to pause at the door. "Don't get too many mountain men down here anymore. What's your business in Temperance?"

Beckett turned his head but kept his hat down so his face was hidden from the deputy. "My business is none of yours."

"Well now, that may be true but as sheriff's deputy I have to warn you, if your business in any way harms this town, I will make it my business."

"Just goin' in for a drink," Beckett turned to enter the Saloon.

"I see you don't carry a gun. Is that knife on your hip your only weapon or do you have a pistol hidden somewhere else on your person?"

"Don't mean no trouble. Just want a drink."

"It's not that we ban guns here, armed men are definitely something I can handle, just prefer you check in with the sheriff's office if you are carrying one."

"All I got's this knife."

"I certainly hope so for your sake, mountain man. Please enjoy your drink and welcome to Temperance." Cincinnati's smile was more menacing than welcoming as he returned to watching the Chinamen.

Beckett hesitated for a second before pushing through the batwings, noticing his hand was clenched so hard there was no feeling in it.

Sherman Saloon was as large and as lavish as a place could be in a dirty mining town. The entrance was at the front corner of the building. Straight back to the left was the bar and to the right were poker tables. In the far corner were stairs that led to rooms to rent and next to them was a piano and a door to the kitchen. The walls and floor were built of warped boards that creaked when Beckett crossed them. Two windows, one on either side of the front door, lit the room. The walls were mostly bare except for a large, double barrel shotgun mounted above a long mirror behind the bar. Beckett took a seat on a stool and threw his saddlebag onto the empty bar. He sat sideways so he could keep his eye on the room and the front door.

Not ten seconds later, Morgan Sherman came out of the kitchen with an armful of clean glasses. He was in his early sixties with long thinning hair and a worn face. His round, red nose sat atop a large, bushy mustache. He was stocky and carried a large belly in front of him. He not only owned and ran Sherman Saloon, he was also the town doctor. Most everyone called him "Doc."

"Beckett! When the hell'd you get here?" Doc said, hastily setting the glasses on the bar.

"Been sitting here for at least twenty minutes now. 'Bout to hop back there and fix myself a drink."

"Why didn't you, you lazy bastard?" Doc said, shaking Beckett's hand. "How've you been?"

"I'm good, Doc." Beckett nodded towards the door. "Quite the maniac you got out there."

"You must mean Sheriff's Deputy Cincinnati." Doc shoved his thumb behind his belt and leaned against the bar in a mocking manner. "He's just trying to keep the town safe, don't you know?"

"Who's gonna keep it safe from him?"

"Well, that's the job of our goddamned benevolent savior, Sheriff Walter Cain. He hung a star on that asshole out there and his two hell spawn sons."

"Ain't had the pleasure of meeting them yet."

"Who, Mordecai and Eli? Well, you're missing out. Good ol' Mord would cave your face in just as soon as look at you and his brother Eli, well … half the whores down at Rick's place have had his pecker forced on them then got beat for the trouble. Had to stitch them up myself. Real saints those two."

"I hear this Cain is some kind of big shot miner."

"Oh, yes," Doc said in a billowy voice Beckett assumed was meant to mimic the sheriff. "Got himself mines all over the Northwest. Started down in California buying up land and taking over towns. Has a whole operation going. Heard his oldest son runs most of them now. Got some mean sounding biblical name too. Cain just likes the power. Likes to play God to us simple folk."

"Apparently likes his deputies shooting men down in the street, too."

"Poor Byron didn't deserve to die like that. Tried to calm him down but the more I did, the more worked up he got. Next time Cain comes in my joint, I'm gonna tell that son of a bitch—"

"Morgan!" a voice yelled from the kitchen door.

Doc's wife Georgia was standing with her hands on her hips in the doorway glaring at her husband. She was about a decade younger than Doc and was a real firecracker. She had long dark hair streaked with waves of silver. She was short and curvy and walked with an attitude.

"I told you to watch your cussing in front of customers," she said, making a beeline for Beckett. "Especially the good looking ones."

She grabbed Beckett by the cheeks and pulled him into an exaggerated kiss on the lips that ended with a loud "muh" sound.

"Well, if it isn't Beckett," she said, hopping onto his lap."How you been, gorgeous?"

"Just fine," he said blushing.

"You got that right."

"Georgia, I ain't running no whorehouse. No need to flaunt your shit in front of the customers."

"Damn it, Morgan, I told you to watch your cussing. Besides, Beckett ain't no regular customer. He's special."

"You two got something going on I don't know about?"

Beckett eased Georgia off his lap." Not that anyone's told me."

"Well, it's been a little longer than your usual three months, Mr. Beckett. Why you been avoiding us?" she said, straightening her bright red dress.

"Ain't been avoidin' you. Just lost track of time."

"You got one of them Coeur d'Alene Indian squaws you been giving it to up in that cabin of yours?" Georgia leered at him.

Beckett flushed again. "Nope, no squaw. Just ain't been keepin' track of time is all."

"Well, it's better late than never," she said to Beckett. "Doc, why ain't you poured this poor man a drink yet?"

"Ain't had a chance with you riding him and all."

"Well, while you're getting over all that, I'm gonna make Mr. Beckett some food," she turned to Beckett. "I could make you a couple of steaks."

"You still got that old hen back there? Was lookin' forward to some eggs if'n you got 'em. Get plenty of meat up in them mountains."

"Sure do. I'll go scramble up a half dozen for you. Gotta keep you fit." She smacked Beckett's rear then spun on her heels and glided into the kitchen.

"I try to keep that woman under control but it's no use," Doc said. "She does make the customers happy though."

"You are one lucky man, Doc."

"So, what'll you have, whiskey?"

"What kind of beer you got back there?"

"Well, got the German stuff in bottles you usually have but I got something else you might like. Ordered a cask of ale on the last stage run. Darker than the bottled stuff and strong. Miners around here won't drink it but I bet you'll love it."

Beckett smiled, enjoying the sales pitch. "Sure, Doc. Sounds good."

"Alright! One ale comin' up."

Doc swiped one of the clean glasses he'd just placed on the bar and slid over to an oak barrel sitting on the far end.

"Your boys still in town?" Beckett asked.

"Sure. Patrick still keeps the place up, cleaning tables and sweeping and such. Don't know why he ain't out here now that you mention it." He turned and yelled to the back, "Patrick! Get the hell out here and get to work, goddamn it!"

Doc placed the glass at an slight angle below the spigot on the oak barrel. He turned the key and a deep amber liquid spilled out. It slowly filled the glass forming a creamy foam head at the top.

"Lucas been running his own delivery business. Doing pretty damned well at it too. Don't see him much on account of he's running between here and Coeur d'Alene most days."

He slid the foamy glass of beer in front of Beckett.

"There you go, genuine English ale."

Beckett took a sip. He could tell the foam had coated the hair on his upper lip. The beer was smooth and slightly sweet. It had a mild bitter aftertaste and more flavor than he was used to but not in a bad way.

Doc stood there waiting for a verdict.

"I like it."

"You do?"

"Sure. It's different."

"Of course it is. These other assholes don't know what they're missing do they?"

Patrick Sherman came in from the back door of the saloon. He was in his late teens with a greasy face and a flop of red hair.

"Where you been, boy?" Doc said. "You out there ogling the girls down at Rick's again?"

"Just had to relieve myself is all, Pa," As Patrick picked up a broom he nodded to Beckett, "Howdy, Mr. Beckett."

Beckett nodded back. "Patrick."

As Beckett took another sip, the batwings swung open and a young black man in a bowler hat hurried in.

"I'm so sorry Doc," he said, catching his breath. "I don't mean to be late. It's just ... that big deputy ..."

"Don't worry about it, Nat," Doc cut him off. "Come on over here. I want you to meet someone."

The man slowed and composed himself. He straightened up and approached the bar. He wore a pressed white shirt with a shiny orange vest and matching sleeve garters.

He was clean shaven except for a pair of wide sideburns that crossed his thin face.

"Beckett, this here is Mr. Nat Harris, best piano player this side of the Rockies. Hired him a few months back to justify having that old noise box back there. He's really livened up the place."

Nat shook Beckett's hand. His fingers were long and thin but he had a strong grip. When he squeezed, the tendons popped out under his dark skin.

He flashed a warm and honest smile at Beckett. "Pleasure to meet you."

"Beckett lives up in those mountains. Comes down here every few months to ... hell, what is it you do down here, Beckett?" Doc said.

"Supplies mostly. And beer."

"More of a fan of gin myself but I can always find time for a good beer," Nat said. "Looks like Doc sold you on his barrel of ale or whatever he calls it."

"It's an English ale and Beckett happens to like it," Doc said.

"That true?" Nat said.

"Sure," Beckett took another sip. "Got a lot of flavor."

"See? At least someone around here's got some taste." Doc said.

"Well, Mr. Beckett, since you came all the way down here for a drink, is there a song you just itchin' to hear, too?" Nat motioned toward the piano.

"Oh, I don't know. Don't follow music much."

"But you gotta have a song you like. I know 'em all. Try me."

"How 'bout Silver Moon? Always liked that one."

"Roll On Silver Moon it is," Nat said, slapping the bar.

He walked over to the piano, sat down and placed his hands on the keys. The jangly tone of the out-of-tune upright echoed off the empty walls of the large room.

"*As I strayed from my cot at the close of the day* ..." Nat's voice was smooth and practiced. He sang with a confidence as though performing for a full room.

Beckett smiled and took another sip of his beer.

"Got him banging away on that thing already?" Georgia said with a plate full of food. "Poor fella's gonna blow his voice out by the end of the night."

She sat the plate in front of Beckett.

"Here you go, darling. Six eggs, scrambled and fresh made bread with orange marmalade."

"Wow, this looks great, Georgia. Thanks."

"My pleasure, good looking." She winked at him as she again, patted his rear.

Beckett finished the plate not long after the song ended. Nat continued playing without singing, saving his voice for a long night of entertaining.

"How long you planning on staying in town?" Doc asked, polishing the bar.

"Couple of days I guess. Headin' out to Frank Gibson's place tonight."

"The old fella who runs the old Fargo way station?"

Beckett nodded. "Me and him got some business."

"Seems like you head out there every time you're in town."

"Known Frank for a long time. Only place'll pay a fair price for fur these days. Trades 'em with the Indians."

"Lucas deals with him quite regular. His station is along one of his delivery routes. Good man."

Beckett finished his beer. "Actually, wanted to talk to you about some business too, if you're interested."

"Possibly. Always interested in a way to make a buck. What you got lined up?"

"I want to sell my claim."

SIX

SHERIFF WALTER CAIN'S OFFICE was above the new bank instead of in the jail next door. It was a large, sparsely furnished and uninviting room that smelled of raw pine and sawdust. There were two modest sized windows that looked out onto Williams Street and two on the southern wall that lit the room quite well in the early afternoon sun. Cain's desk at the back of the room was made of flamed maple with a deep red stain. Facing the desk in the middle of the room were two high-backed chairs constructed of ornately carved rosewood with back and seat pads made of a dark blue fabric that shimmered in the light. The furniture was as new as the room.

Sheriff Cain sat behind the desk, wearing a hat made of a dark burgundy leather that curled on the edge. He was in his sixties, lean but not thin and wore a tailored, Italian made three-piece suit. A gold chain draped from the pocket of his vest and was attached to a buttonhole with a diamond encrusted pin. His facial hair was immaculately trimmed into a style popular with southern aristocrats yet he spoke with no discernible accent. Across from him sat two deputies, one gaunt and tall and the other much larger and thicker.

"That's not the answer I was hoping for, Eli," he said to the gaunt deputy. "You assured me you would be ready in two days."

"Well now, Pa, when I told you that, I didn't know that certain problems would arise." Eli gnawed on the nail of his left thumb while his knee bounced with nervous energy. "We'll get it done, it's just that the fellas are runnin' a little behind."

"So, now you're telling me the men you're in charge of, the men who take orders from you are the reason our timetable is now completely fucked." His voice was calm yet had an unnerving effect on Eli.

"I'll get on 'em, Pa. We'll get it done."

"Now, that's what I like to hear." The sheriff relaxed back in his chair. "And I can only assume that you're going to get your ass back there and personally oversee these men who have been shirking their responsibilities under your command. I mean, if in two days we are still behind schedule I can't possibly punish every man at the mine. It will be much more efficient if I just reprimand their superior."

"Guess so."

"Good, then I guess you'd better get going. I'll send Cincinnati up in the morning to check on your progress. I have something else for him to take care of while he's out there."

"I won't let you down Pa." Eli bounced up out of his chair as though full of pent up energy.

"I know you won't son." The sheriff smiled. "You know … or else."

Eli quickly left the office by way of the stairs leading down to the bank.

"You see, Mordecai, your younger brother can be productive with the right motivation," Sheriff Cain said to the remaining deputy.

"He's still a complete fuck up."

"True, but when I leave and take Cincinnati with me, you'll be the one who's going to have to keep him in line."

"Don't know why you're stickin' me with him."

"Because I think it'll be good for you boys. Help you build some camaraderie."

Sheriff Cain stood up, walked to one of the front windows and looked out onto Williams Street, catching Eli as he stomped out of the front of the bank and hoisted himself up onto his horse. As he reined the animal violently out into the street, he yelled at two men standing in front of the bank.

"Come on, you sorry sacks of shit. We goin' back to the goddamn mine and fix what you assholes gone and fucked up."

Sheriff Cain rolled his eyes and turned back to his desk. He popped the cork on a bottle of whiskey and pulled two glasses from a drawer. He splashed some of the amber liquid into them and handed one to Mordecai.

"Now, what were you in such a hurry to tell me when you walked in on my talk with young Eli?"

"Well, I just got done talking to Cincinnati and I think we might have a problem."

"What kind of problem?"

"So, I guess while I was gone doin' my shakedowns, our trigger happy lead deputy went and shot down some asshole in the street for talking back to him. "

"I'm sure Deputy Cincinnati was well within his legal rights. Why is that a problem?"

"It ain't. The problem is I guess some mountain man saw the whole thing and Cincinnati thinks he's going to be trouble."

"Did this mountain man do anything?"

"No. Cincinnati says he can just tell."

"He can. That's why I hired him."

"Well, I did some checking around and this mountain man is a fella called Beckett who owns the claim west of site three."

"I thought you had already acquired that claim."

"No, we've been goin' after the ones to the north and heading that way. I was gonna roust him next week but after what Cincinnati says, 'bout how he can tell this Beckett is trouble, I don't think my usual methods will work."

"What do you think will persuade him, Mordecai?"

"Don't know. Haven't seen the guy in person. Don't know exactly what I'm dealing with, just what Cincinnati thinks."

Sheriff Cain pounded his glass of whiskey on the desk. "We need that claim, Mordecai. Site three is more promising than one and two combined. I don't care what it takes."

"I know, Pa. I'll get it."

"Where is this Beckett now?"

"Cincinnati says he's over at Sherman's."

"Well, why don't you go over there and see exactly what we're dealing with? You should have done that before you even came to me."

Mordecai stood up to leave.

"And take Cincinnati with you. Just in case he's right."

SEVEN

"I CAN'T AFFORD no goddamn gold claim, Beckett. Even if it ain't got no gold on it," Doc said. "Don't know why you came to me anyway. Sheriff Cain's been buying up every claim along the river."

He and Beckett had retreated to the alley behind Sherman Saloon to talk in private and so Doc could have a cigar without Georgia getting on him. Beckett stood with his saddlebag over his shoulder.

"Don't want to sell it to him. I want to sell it to you."

"I ain't got that kind of money, I told you," Doc said, puffing his cigar.

"Not lookin' for money. You see, the claim, the cabin and even my horse were given to me by the previous owner. I ain't got nothin' into it except for a coat made of buffalo so I'm not expecting anything out of it."

Doc choked on the smoke "Wait. Are you tellin' me you want to give me the claim?"

"Less the price of a coat made of buffalo. I think about twenty dollars would cover it. Oh, and my sorrel ain't part of the deal no more neither. Kind of like him."

"You want to sell me your twenty-acre gold claim for twenty dollars?"

"Yes. You interested?"

Doc put his cigar out against the building and dropped it into the pocket of his shirt.

"Shit, Beckett, I can't take your gold claim for nothing."

"You're not. You're giving me twenty dollars for it. Besides, I've already been in this argument. I know how it will end."

"I don't know how to feel about this."

"Well, when you figure out how you feel, just do me one thing. Make sure Cain comes nowhere near it."

"Why are you so against selling to Cain? I mean, he's a goddamn son of a bitch and deserves to rot in hell, you ask me, but you don't even know the man."

"I see what he's doing to this town. I've known men like him before. They take what they want because they can and leave nothing for anybody else." Beckett paused for a beat. "I only knew the man who gave me the claim for a short time but he was one to leave an impression. That claim and the cabin on it mean a lot to me. I don't want a man like Cain to have it."

"But why me? Why don't you give it to your buddy down at the way station?"

"Frank wouldn't want it. Besides, he's old and crippled and wouldn't be able to protect it. I figure you and your boys can work it and keep men like Cain away."

Doc put out a hand and leaned against the building, looking consternated. Beckett wondered if this is what he looked like when Oliver Crow had given him the claim.

"Well, I can't say no can I?"

"Nope."

Doc stood, looking Beckett in the eyes.

"Fine. I'll take your claim. I only have one condition," Doc straightened up and crossed his arms over his large belly trying to appear firm. "If me and my boys work that claim and there is any gold up there, I'm splitting it with you fifty, fifty. "

"Deal," Beckett said spitting into his hand.

Doc did likewise before shaking with Beckett.

Beckett pulled a folded-up piece of paper from his saddlebag and handed it to Doc. "That's the deed for the claim. Already signed it over to you. You can give me the twenty dollars next time I see you."

"You are one crazy son of a bitch, Beckett."

"That's what I hear."

"What you selling for anyway? You moving on?"

"Got something I've gotta take care of. Somethin' that's been a long time comin'."

"Well, whatever that something is, I think it calls for a drink."

As Doc and Beckett reentered Sherman Saloon through the rear door, they noticed the lively atmosphere that filled the room before they left had been replaced by tension and a sense of foreboding. Nat was no longer playing piano and was standing out of sight by the stairs. The few customers who had been playing poker were now quietly sitting and looking down at their drinks.

At the front door, Cincinnati stood with a thumb behind his belt buckle, leaning against the frame just like he'd been in front of the sheriff's office. He nodded at Beckett.

Georgia stood behind the bar polishing a glass with a rag. She glared at the only man sitting at the bar.

"You must be Beckett," the man at the bar said standing up. He was a full foot taller than Beckett and at least a hundred pounds heavier. He was a big man but he wasn't fat, just huge. His hat was curved at the end and had a short crown. His head was round and made his eyes and mouth look tiny. A week's worth of stubble covered his chin. In his holster was an ebony-handled Navy Colt that looked small against his frame. A brass star was pinned to his suede vest.

Beckett walked into the middle of the room and stood, facing the man. He casually rested the ball of his hand on the heel of his Bowie.

"On behalf of the sheriff's department, I'd like to welcome you to Temperance. My name is Deputy Mordecai Cain."

"Told your pal at the door I ain't lookin' for no trouble."

"Well, now," Mordecai said, trying to act insulted. "That ain't no way to act towards a fella who's just trying to be friendly."

"Ain't lookin' to be your friend neither."

Mordecai eased away from the bar and moved within inches of Beckett. Beckett didn't look up at him.

"Cincinnati here tells me you're trouble," Mordecai said in a lower tone. "Well, I'm here to tell you if you do anything in this town but play by our rules, you won't leave it alive."

The brim of Beckett's hat failed to block the rancid breath of the big man.

"Got me, friend?"

Beckett avoided Mordecai's eyes.

"You hear me?" Mordecai said, raising his voice. "I asked you a question."

Beckett took two steps back so he was able to look the huge Deputy in the eye.

"I heard you. I just couldn't understand what you said. You see, my clodhopper is a little rusty."

Mordecai looked at him quizzically before his eyes went wide and his face turned crimson.

"You son of a ..." Mordecai reached for Beckett's collar with his left hand.

Beckett's right shot up and caught him on the wrist, squeezing it with a power he could tell Mordecai wasn't expecting. The huge deputy reared back and swung his right fist. Beckett's left hand caught the punch in mid-flight. For a split second the two stood in the middle of the room like dancing partners. In a quick movement, Beckett jerked his head back, losing his hat with the effort, then straightened his torso and neck, thrusting forward and upward, using the full force of his legs to smash his forehead into Mordecai's nose. Blood exploded from Mordecai's face as he stumbled backward. He cupped his splintered nose then looked down at the blood pouring from it.

"You broke my fucking nose!" he yelled.

Beckett stood back with his hand on his bowie as Mordecai drew his Army revolver.

"Mordecai!" Cincinnati yelled from the doorway. "This is not the time."

"Did you see what this asshole did to my face?"

"Holster your piece and let's go."

Mordecai stood with his gun drawn, pointing it toward the floor. Beckett stared him down with his hand still on his Bowie.

Cincinnati grabbed the injured deputy's arm. "Mordecai. Let's go!"

"You're fucking dead, mountain man." Mordecai holstered his revolver as he backed away pulled by Cincinnati out the door.

"Oh, and Sherman," Mordecai said through gurgling blood. "You'd better keep your nigger out of the street. If I see him out front again, I'm gonna skin him."

A warm afternoon breeze poured in as the batwings swung closed.

Everyone remained frozen in place, staring at Beckett. A spot of blood on his forehead trickled down the bridge of his nose. As he wiped it away with his hand, Georgia held out a clean washrag to him.

"Are you bleeding?"

Beckett took the rag from her and wiped his face. "Don't think so."

"I can't believe what I just saw." She leaned forward against the bar, her face beaming. "Beckett, you are the only man I've ever seen that stood up to those assholes and survived."

"Georgia, watch your language." Doc said.

"If the whole town did that, Cain and his boys wouldn't stand a chance." Georgia slapped the bar with the flat of her hand to emphasize the point.

"Didn't do nothin' I couldn't get myself out of," Beckett said. "Only one language men like that understand."

"Oh, no," she said. "This was different. Poor Byron was the last man to stand up to one of them and he didn't stand a chance. I saw that Deputy Cincinnati just now. When you did what you did, for a second there was a flash of fear in his eyes."

"I saw it too," said a man who had been standing in the back by the poker tables. "Never seen them boys back off like that. You ain't even got a gun."

The man was obviously a miner. He had a dilapidated hat and dusty clothes. The only thing that set him apart from every other miner in town was a huge Walker Colt revolver on his hip.

The miner walked over to Beckett's hat on the floor, picked it up and handed it to him. "Name's Harvey Coleman. Let me buy you a drink."

"Thanks. I think I could use one," Beckett touched his forehead and felt swelling before replacing his hat.

He sat at the bar in the same position as when he first arrived. The saddlebag, which had never left his shoulder throughout the encounter with Mordecai, went back on the bar.

Harvey Coleman sat on the stool next to him. "Two whiskeys please, Georgia. And leave the bottle."

She grabbed a bottle and poured their drinks. Doc slid behind the bar and took a place next to his wife.

"'Bout damn time them assholes got put in their place." Harvey took a drink and poured himself another. "Cain stole my claim a few months back. Ask him and he'd tell you he bought it fair and square. Well, there's nothin' fair and square about havin' a gun to your head, takin' pennies on the dollar for your livelihood. Them bastards forced me off my land. Worst part is, I can't afford to move on so I had to take a job at one of Cain's mines up north. Son of a bitch pretty much owns me."

"Harvey ain't the only one neither," Doc said. "The town's full of folks in the same position."

"Cain is a monster. 'Course his boys are even worse," Harvey said. "Look at how Mord treats poor Nat. I don't give a shit what color he is. Man's a fine piano player and a fine human being and don't deserve the hell that clodhopper, as you put it, dishes out."

"Pretty much can't walk down the streets no more with them around," Nat said, emerging from the back. "Have to go out the back and sneak through the alleys."

Beckett took a sip of his whiskey. As he looked around the room all eyes were upon him. "Don't take much. Just got to stand up to them. Don't back down."

"Easy for you to say," Harvey said.

"Nothin' easy about it."

"'Course if you carried one of these, you could probably run them off for good," Harvey set his revolver on the bar with a metallic thud. "That's an original Walker Colt. Not one of the newer, lighter Dragoons neither. This monster weighs almost five pounds. Most powerful handgun made. At a couple yards, it'll take a man's head clean off. A fella your size should be carrying one of these."

"I do just fine with my Bowie." Beckett touched the big knife at his side then nodded at the gun on the bar. "If you're so good with that thing, why don't you take Sheriff Cain down? Hell, Doc's got that huge, ten-gauge scattergun over the bar. You both could make a run at him."

"Well, now, I ain't no gunman. Don't figure Doc is neither," Harvey backpedaled. "Guess you'd say I'm more of a collector."

"Harvey's right, Beckett. Even if we were armed to the teeth, we wouldn't be able to stand up to Cain and his men like you did," Doc said.

"Well, maybe you should try." Beckett finished his whiskey. "Now, if you'll excuse me, I've got someplace to be."

He stood up, threw his saddlebag over his shoulder and tossed a few coins onto the bar. He nodded to Georgia then to Doc.

"Pleasure to meet you fellas," Beckett said nodding to Nat and Harvey.

"You too," they said in unison.

Beckett checked his throbbing forehead one more time then swung through the batwings.

EIGHT

BECKETT RODE SOUTH through the mountains toward a valley halfway between Temperance and a town called Wallace. The walk from Sherman Saloon to his horse and mule had been uneventful. Both deputy Cincinnati and deputy Mordecai were nowhere to be seen. He'd said goodbye to Samuel, who'd been waiting by his sorrel, and exited Temperance the way he'd entered.

As soon as the town was behind him, a pair of glossy, dark eyes appeared in the trees to his right.

"Come on, boy," Beckett said, encouraging the dog but not expecting any response. To his surprise, the dog bounded from the darkness and fell in step six feet behind Beckett's trailing mule. He looked back at the animal and smiled. As he breathed in the warm mountain air, the tension of his encounter in Temperance completely left him.

An hour into his ride he stopped at a stream to let the animals drink. The late afternoon heat brought out cicadas that hummed a chorus around him. As he filled his canteen, he noticed the mutt sitting at attention right behind him.

"You want more jerky?"

The dog's white-tipped tail answered with a back and forth flick, stirring pine needles.

Beckett reached into his saddlebag and pulled out another chunk of dried meat. The dog's tail moved vigorously, scattering more needles.

"Okay, but you have to come to me to get it," he said, holding the piece of meat out in front of him.

The dog lowered its perked ears and nosed forward cautiously. It hesitated every other step before pausing a couple of feet from Beckett's hand.

"It's okay. I won't hurt you."

The dog's eyes met Beckett's. Slowly the distance between man and animal narrowed until the mutt finally snatched the jerky from Beckett's hand. It retreated a few paces before eating the meat then returned to attention.

Beckett laughed, "Nope, that's it for now. I have a feeling you'd clean me out if I gave you the chance."

The white-tipped tail stirred needles at Beckett's words.

"Alright, boys. Let's get going." He mounted his sorrel and guided his horse and mule across the shallow stream back through the ponderosa pines. The mutt plodded across after him, falling in place alongside.

An hour later the pines began to thin and a shallow, diamond-shaped valley appeared below him. Bushes and low grass blanketed soft rolling green hills across the valley's quarter-mile length. In the center of the diamond sat a wood-paneled stable next to a modest cabin with a huge pine tree outside its rear door. Two dirt roads converged in the middle of the valley, one running from the trees on the west, the other exiting to the south. The cabin's entrance faced southwest at the junction of the two roads, providing a full view of both.

Beckett rode from the northern point of the valley along the tree line until he reached the road from the west. The sorrel's metal shoes clicked on the bare rocks of the road and kicked up low dust clouds that the mottled grey mutt veered to avoid.

As he neared the junction of the two roads, he pulled up in front of a stable on his left. The structure was two stories tall with two large doors that opened wide enough to fit a stagecoach. The walls were made of warped pine boards and the gabled roof was covered with broken shake shingles. Inside he could see a brown gelding and a beautiful palomino mare with an ivory snout tied to a hitch. They grazed on a thick layer of hay covering the sawdust floors.

The grey mutt hung back, using the stable to block its view of the cabin while keeping Beckett in its sights as he slid from his sorrel, looping the reins around a hitch outside. The horse snorted at the animals in the stable while Beckett unhooked the mule's lead from his saddle and tied it off.

"You better not be no road agent lookin' to rob and kill me," a stern voice called from the doorway of the cabin. "Wouldn't want to have to come over there and snap your neck with my bare hands."

A man stood on the covered wooden porch in front of the cabin, a gnarled cane supporting his weight. He was small and thin with grey hair and a beard that was almost white.

"I'd like to see you try, old man," Beckett tossed his saddlebag over his shoulder.

"Don't push me, Beckett. I may be an old cripple but I can still take you."

Beckett climbed the steps, staring the old man down. He received a glare in return until the old man sniggered.

"I'm gonna let you off the hook this time." The old man took Beckett's outstretched hand then pulled him in for a hug. "But next time you're dead."

"Good to see you, Frank." Beckett's voice was louder than usual, knowing the old man was hard of hearing.

"Good to see you too, kid."

"How you been gettin' along?"

"I hobble here and there but I get by. You're lookin' ... well, huge. Is that solid muscle?" Frank jabbed a finger into Beckett's chest. "What you been doin' up in them mountains?"

"Cuttin' trees. Haulin' dirt. Killin' bears. You know, mountain man stuff."

"Bah, you ain't no mountain man, Beckett."

"No, but I can pretend can't I?"

"*Pretend.* That's a good word for it."

"Well, you must be doin' better than you let on. I see that you've taken down that pine out front." Beckett gestured toward a fresh stump a couple yards from the front porch. "Looks like you did some repairs to the roof too. You got Chinamen coming down here to help you out?"

"Nah, Abigail been takin' care of most of that. Under my strict supervision of course."

"Abigail?" Beckett cracked a smile. "You didn't go and get married again did you, Frank?"

"Oh, God no," a voice said from behind him. "Daddy ain't the marrying type. Even he knows that."

Beckett turned to see a young woman leaning on an axe handle. She was in her early twenties, with a wiry build. Her wavy, auburn hair fell below her shoulders and framed her face. Long hours in the sun had made her skin golden, the perfect background for her large green eyes and long, dark eyelashes. A blue checkered, gingham dress clung to her curves and was unbuttoned at the top, revealing a hint of bosom framed in lace. Beckett was so taken aback by her appearance he almost didn't notice the dual, pearl-handled Colts she wore on a gun belt resting on her hips.

"You can call me Abby. Only Daddy calls me Abigail."

"Name's Beckett," he said, removing his hat. "Pleasure."

"Abigail's been helpin' out 'round here past few months. Her mother sent her up after my accident.

"What accident?"

"Oh, nothin' I couldn've handled."

"He fell off the roof and almost broke his neck this spring." Abby smirked as she shook her head. "Man from the stage came across him a day later and hauled him to a doctor in Wallace. That's when he wired my mother. Seein' as she was all upset that I ain't found no husband yet and I ain't got no prospects, she sent me up here from Helena to lend a hand. Momma'd never admit it but she's still in love with the old cripple."

"She can stay in Montana for all I care," Frank said.

"That's Daddy's way of sayin' he still loves her too." She nodded at Beckett's right hand. "By the way, you can put that back on your head. I won't be offended."

Beckett looked down to see he was holding his hat. He had no idea he'd removed it or when. His attempt to casually return it to his head was met by a smile from the young woman.

Beckett turned to Frank. "In all the years I've known you, you've never mentioned you had a daughter.

"Never came up I guess." Frank shrugged.

Beckett whipped back to look at Abby standing with her axe. "Wait. You tellin' me that you cut down that big pine by yourself?"

"Cuttin' it down wasn't no problem and haulin' it off with the pack horse was a breeze. Ain't had the chance to cut it into rounds and split it though," she said. "It's around back if'n you and your big arms are plannin' on stayin'."

"I was hopin' to stay the night if that's okay. Be happy to do some work while I'm here."

"We'd be insulted if you didn't stay," Frank said. "Got some catchin' up to do."

Beckett's gaze remained on Abby. "That we do."

NINE

IT WAS EVENING when Beckett closed up the stable. He'd unsaddled his horse and brushed it, removed the furs, pack and gear from his mule then fed and watered both animals. It took two trips to bring everything to the cabin. On the second, he looked for the mutt. The dog alertly sat at the corner of the stable but was unwilling to come any closer to the cabin. Beckett didn't push it. He threw the dog a large piece of meat he'd brought from inside. The animal snatched it and took it behind the stable.

Walking in the front door of the cabin with his roll of furs over his shoulder, he asked where he should put them.

"Just drop them by the door." Frank sat in a rickety, old rocking chair, holding a tin cup full of whiskey. "Caught yourself a bear?"

"Yup. Told you I got this mountain man thing down."

"You break down and use a rifle?"

"Nope. Just my Bowie."

"Bullshit."

"Seriously. Trapped him, lassoed him and cut his throat."

Frank laughed.

Beckett took another tin cup and filled it from the bottle next to Frank before sitting in a chair facing the door.

"Did you say you killed that bear without a gun?" Abby was by the fireplace, throwing herbs into a small metal pot hanging above the burning logs. "Why would you do that?"

"Exactly," Frank said. "Why would anyone do that?"

"More of a challenge that way," Beckett took a swig from the cup which he held by the curved handle since the bottom was slightly rusted.

Abby stirred the pot with a long wooden spoon before dishing up a small amount for a sip. "You forget your rifle at home?"

"Oh, Beckett don't carry no gun. Just that huge guttin' knife on his hip. Got a hatchet on his saddle too if'n I recall," Frank said. "He's like a goddamned Injun that way. 'Course even the savages use Winchesters now days."

"But it makes absolutely no sense trappin' bear without a rifle."

"Sense never came into it. Just the way I do things is all." Beckett nodded at Abby's waist. "I see you ain't hurtin' for firepower. Them six-guns look bigger than you."

"Well, they ain't there for show." She removed the pot from the fire, setting it on a table in the corner. "A girl needs to be able to protect herself in the wilds of the West."

"And this girl knows how to use 'em. She can shoot a flea off the back of a coyote runnin'," Frank said. "And she's fast."

"The word 'fast' can be very subjective." Beckett leaned forward in his chair and rested his elbows on his knees. "I've seen fellas who thought they were fast get lit up by a gunman who—"

In one fluid motion, Abby drew her left pistol. An explosion was followed by a metallic clang and a spray of whiskey across the back wall. She stood there with the Colt smoking in her hand, a smirk on her face.

"Damn it, Abigail!" Frank said. "That was my good Kentucky bourbon."

Beckett looked at the floor near the back wall where his cup dripped liquid from two new holes, one on each side.

"And that was with my bad hand." Abby blew across the shiny nickel barrel of her gun and spun it back into its holster.

Beckett remained quiet, eyeing her with a curious smile. She matched his gaze and gave him a playful grin.

Frank interrupted the interplay. "Them's the new dual action, Colts. Gun rep came by here few months back and sold 'em to me. Calls them the Colt Thunderer. I gave 'em to Abigail to replace her old hand-me-down Remingtons." Frank beamed. Beckett wasn't sure whether the old man's obvious pride was for Abby or the guns. "Don't need to cock the hammer to shoot 'em. Abigail here can empty all twelve rounds before you can blink."

"Fascinating." Beckett sat up and turned his eyes back to Abby.

Noticing the direction of his gaze, Frank thrust a bowl at Beckett. "Rabbit stew is ready. Eat up before it gets cold." Having caught Beckett's attention, Frank offered a wry smile and nodded Abby's way as if saying, "Watch yourself with my daughter." As he dished up a bowl he said, "Abigail, get our guest another whiskey."

* * *

AFTER THEY ATE, Frank retreated to one of the two small rooms toward the back of the cabin. Beckett went outside and sat on a carved bench on the porch, lighting up a cigar Frank had given him. He sipped whiskey from a new cup as he looked up at the stars that lit the clear moonless night sky. The liquor, the warm September breeze and the hum of crickets were lulling and his eyes gradually closed.

"Daddy really likes you." Beckett's eyelids opened to see Abby, leaning against the deck railing across from him, her gun belt no longer on her hips. She looked beautiful and mysterious in the flickering firelight coming from the fireplace through the window, the only illumination on the porch other than the stars. "Never known him to speak so fondly 'bout anyone."

"Known Frank a long time. Helped me get out of a dark place some years back. Offered me a job in Seattle before I headed out into the mountains. He's a good man."

"What are you doin' in them mountains anyway? You runnin' away from something?"

Beckett took a puff on his cigar, "Ain't we all runnin' away from somethin'?"

She looked at him, raising one eyebrow, "You ain't no cold blooded killer in hidin' are you?"

He took another swig, "What happened to your peace-makers?"

"Didn't figure I needed them with a brute like you hangin' 'round."

"What's a girl like you really need them for anyway? You got somethin' to prove?"

"Nah, just like to make men nervous. Keep 'em guessin'. Momma says it's account of my revolvers why I can't find a husband."

"You lookin' for one?"

"You offering?"

"Wasn't in my evenin' plans."

Abby smiled and played with the hem on the sleeve of her dress. Her fingers were thin and strong. For a few moments she was quiet, as though preoccupied with a thought.

"Never really wanted one, tell you the truth." She turned her head and looked off in the distance. "Seen how my folks got along when they was together. They get along a lot better livin' in different territories. How 'bout you? You got a wife?"

"Had one."

"She leave you for bein' ornery?" Abby smirked.

"She died."

"Oh, shit, I'm sorry." She folded her hands over her heart as she turned and looked at him. Beckett thought the genuine concern in her big eyes was intoxicating. "I was just tryin' to make a joke. I didn't know—"

"It was a long time ago." His tone was reassuring.

"Did you love her?"

"Sure. Had to've I guess. Consumption took her a few years in. I was runnin' cattle when she got sick. By the time I got word and made it back she was gone."

Even in the shadows, Beckett could see tears forming in the corners of Abby's eyes, making them twinkle like the stars above.

"I'm so sorry," she said. "I couldn't even imagine what that would be like."

"Dyin' is somethin' we all gotta do. She just did hers earlier than some."

Beckett drained the rest of his whiskey.

Abby wiped the corners of her eyes and composed herself.

"You ever kill anyone with them six-guns?" Beckett held his thumbs up and his index fingers extended, aiming at Abby. As his thumbs came down, he made an explosive noise from the corner of his mouth and winked at her.

She laughed, "Why, you worried?"

"Guns don't scare me. A pretty gal on the other hand …"

Beckett thought he saw her break into a smile, but was unsure in the waning firelight.

"No, I ain't killed no one. 'Course if someone was to come at me, I'd stop them in their tracks." Abby mimicked him, using her thumb and forefinger to form a gun.

"You think so, huh? You know, shootin' tin cups and shootin' a man are two very different things. When you face down a real gunman for the first time, everything you think you know 'bout shootin' will disappear. If you're lucky, you'll piss yourself and he'll take pity on you. Leave you with a bullet in the arm for the trouble."

"What do you know about it anyway? Don't picture you getting in too many gunfights with that knife on your hip."

"Can't be in a gunfight if'n you ain't got no gun."

"You can get shot in the back, though."

"You can get shot in the back with two Colts on your hip, too." He slid his huge Bowie knife from its holster and turned it, reflecting what little light there was. "Matter of fact you can have your throat cut from behind and no one will hear it."

"But what do you do when you can't sneak up on someone? What do you do if they're standing six feet from you?"

"You mean like from me to you?"

Beckett flipped his knife in the air and caught it near the tip of the blade. He flung it across the porch where it stuck with a thunk in the one-inch space between Abby's feet. She sat speechless, looking down at the elk-horn handle between her ankles.

He took another puff on his cigar. "Probably do that only aim a little higher."

"I'm impressed." She bent over to pick up the knife, grabbing it with one hand. When it wouldn't budge, she tried with both hands and almost fell backwards over the railing when it finally gave.

After regaining her balance, she examined the weapon. The polished blade gleamed as she turned it. The handle was worn and much too big for her hand. She hefted it to determine its weight. "I think I'll stick with my Colts."

"I ain't gonna try and stop you." Beckett held his hand out.

Abby moved closer and handed him the knife. She leaned forward, her big green eyes sparkling with firelight. Her mouth was parted slightly, her soft lips forming a smile.

As he rose from the bench to face her, she turned, her hair bouncing around her shoulders. "I think I'll turn in. You got everything you need?"

Beckett hesitated then said, "Yeah. Thanks."

She moved to the doorway then stopped halfway in. She leaned out with her hand on the door frame.

"Goodnight, Beckett."

"Goodnight, Abby."

***

A HALF HOUR LATER Beckett walked to the stable. He threw his saddle blanket onto the thick hay and lay down, looking up at stars peeking through holes in the roof. Just as he was about to fall asleep, the door to the stable creaked. He propped himself up on his elbows. A small figure squeezed through the narrow opening.

"Come 'ere, boy."

The mottled grey mutt walked over and sniffed Beckett's hand.

"Sorry. Got nothin' for you."

The dog looked him in the eye then circled a few times in the hay. It lay down in a pile next to Beckett's head and gave out a long grunt.

"I feel the same way, buddy," Beckett said.

TEN

THE AIR WAS CRISP and a few stars were still visible as Beckett relieved himself behind the stable. The sun had risen but was still struggling to reach the diamond shaped valley through the tree line to the east. As shafts of sunlight began sneaking between the pines, they cut through the low, morning mist, illuminating patches of grass. *At night the earth is the devil's playground,* his mother used to say. *When the sun rises it brings God's love with it. The beams of light that streak through the trees at dawn are God's fingers.* It was a comforting thought for a small boy who still thought there were monsters and demons out to get him in the night. As that boy grew up though, he realized it was total bullshit. From first hand experience he knew that monsters and demons were just as capable of their sinister deeds in the light.

Beckett returned to his makeshift bed inside the stable, loosened the leather string on his teardrop-shaped bag and removed the wooden box, inkwell and pen. His lantern had about ten minutes of oil left. He placed it on a bail of hay, lit it, pulled a piece of paper from the box and began to write.

The lantern was about to flicker out just as he finished the page. As he read over his writing he felt a presence nearby.

"Got some oats and bacon on the table if'n you're hungry." Her voice was sweeter than he'd remembered. He wasn't sure how long she'd been there. He was usually keenly aware of every detail of his surroundings but when he was writing, the world around him faded away.

"Good morning, Abby."

She smiled. "Good morning, Beckett.

"Thank you. Breakfast sounds great. I'll be in in a moment."

"Alright, then." She eyed his writing utensils then turned and left the stable.

Beckett watched her all the way.

When he was sure the ink was dry he folded the paper, opened his saddlebag and stuffed it in the envelope with the others. Packing up his things, he noticed the grey mutt sitting at attention stirring up hay and sawdust with its white-tipped tail.

"You been sitting here the whole time?"

The mutt's mouth opened a crack, letting its tongue escape one side. It looked like the dog was smiling.

"You must like her too, huh?" Beckett slowly reached to pet the mutt on the head, expecting it to pull away. Instead of flinching, the dog wagged its tail more vigorously.

The mutt's bravery ended once Beckett started for the cabin. It remained in the stable, sniffing for something to eat.

"Looks like I owe you some money," Frank said as Beckett walked inside.

"Why's that? Did we make a bet?"

"No. Your skins. I looked 'em over this morning. Injuns on the res will probably give me a couple months of grain for that bear. Others are good too. Looks like you've finally learned to skin 'em right."

"Had the chance to practice." He placed his saddlebag over the back of a chair. "Need you to take a look at my big trap by the way. It ain't movin' as smoothly as it used to. May need some adjustment."

"Is that right?" Frank's eyes lit up. "Guess I better get my tools and take a look."

Frank pulled himself up from his chair, using his cane for support and hobbled out the door toward the stable.

"He loves tinkerin' with his tools," Abby said, preparing a plate for Beckett. "Especially likes workin' on them traps."

"I know. I always bring them down here for him. I try to be extra hard on them just so he has something to adjust."

He took the plate from her and began to eat. The bacon was blackened and fell apart in his mouth. The oats were rubbery and tasted like liver or whatever had coated the pot previously. He ate without comment, grateful for the company.

They were silent for a few minutes as Abby busied herself around the cabin. Beckett couldn't help but watch. Her movements were strong but graceful in the soft morning light.

"That old pine you cut down, is it out back?"

"Yes, I've limbed it but it needs to be sawed into rounds and split."

He stood up and handed her his empty plate. "Guess I'll get to it then."

"There's a saw hangin' out back. Axe is leaning up against the wood pile."

"I'll find it."

As he headed toward the door, her voice stopped him. "Beckett."

He turned back to her.

"Thanks."

"My pleasure." He smiled and tipped an imaginary hat.

As Beckett started toward the back of the cabin, he heard Frank banging away on something metal in the stable, causing the animals to nervously shuffle around at the noise. The mutt was nowhere to be seen.

He followed the dirt rut that ran from the stump out front until it ended at the base of the downed trunk that lay in the grass under the large pine behind the cabin. He took down the saw from its hook and positioned it on the log about sixteen inches from the base. The saw was four feet long with teeth that looked like metal fangs. It had two wooden handles, one on either end. It was designed to be used by two people but Beckett had no problem cutting through the soft pine by himself.

By late morning, the sun was high enough to begin baking the dusty earth. Beckett was now swinging an axe in his unbuttoned long underwear, having removed his tattered red shirt. Circles of sweat formed below his arms and covered his back. The small pile of wood he'd found the axe leaning against was now twice the size it had been.

As he placed another round onto the chopping block and lifted the axe, he was interrupted by a smooth voice behind him.

"You look like you could use a drink." Abby held a metal pitcher and one of the tin cups he'd drunk whiskey from the night before.

Beckett dropped the head of the axe to the ground and leaned against the handle. He wiped the sweat from his brow with the sleeve of his long underwear.

"I reckon I could."

She filled the cup with well water from the pitcher and handed it to him. He sat back against the wood pile while he drank.

"I can't believe how fast you've gotten through this thing. Would've taken me a whole month to cut up that log."

"Had a lot of experience. Nothin' much to do up in them mountains but chop firewood."

He caught her steeling a glance at his exposed chest. He, in turn, looked at her hips. "You still ain't wearing your Colts?"

"Use 'em for protection. Don't feel like I need 'em with certain folk bein' 'round."

"Certain folk bein' me?'

She smiled.

"Don't know how much protection I can provide with this little ol' knife."

"You proved your point last night. Can't be in a gunfight if'n you ain't got no gun."

"Intimidation gets you a long way. It's like playin' cards. If you're facin' down a fella, make sure he knows you're sure of what you got in your hand, especially if you got nothin'. The fact that you're so confident will make him second guess himself even if he knows he's got four aces."

"I ain't no tall dark and handsome mountain man with a huge knife. How am I supposed to intimidate a gunfighter without pullin' out my Colts?"

"Don't need to pull 'em. The fact that you're a good lookin' gal with a couple of six-guns on your hips is intimidating to most fellas. Trust me." He took another gulp. "Just showin' you got 'em is enough. Ain't got nothin' against you or anyone carryin' guns. Just think that most folk that got 'em are too quick to pull 'em. Honestly, I'd feel better if they were on your hips when I left here tomorrow. Make anyone who was itchin' to mess with you or Frank second guess himself."

"Well, as soon as you and your big arms and your big knife leave us tomorrow, I'll put my intimidation back on my hips."

Beckett laughed, thinking, *Those hips are intimidating enough by themselves.*

"Where you headin' in the morning?"

"Gonna make my way back to town, pick up some supplies and finish some business. Then I'm headin' south."

"You ain't goin' back to your mountain?"

"Nope. Got some stuff to take care of away from here."

He caught the disappointment in her eyes.

"You think you'll be back this way again?"

"Don't rightly know. All I know now is I have to head south."

He stood up and handed the tin cup back to her. "How 'bout you. You gonna stick around with Frank?"

"For now. Don't feel right leavin' him alone the way he is. I know Momma ain't gonna come out here and take my place. Haven't thought much beyond that."

"You know, not everyone ends up like your folks." He picked up the axe. "One of these days you're gonna make some lucky fella real happy despite what your ma thinks."

Abby watched Beckett swing the axe, splintering a log with a single blow.

"Maybe"

ELEVEN

FRANK GIBSON was bent over a wooden pail scrubbing grease from his hands when the men rode up. He saw their long, afternoon shadows blacken the ground around him before he heard the hooves of their horses. He reached for his cane and pulled himself up.

"Good afternoon, Mr. Gibson. Nice to see that you're up and around. That was quite the fall you had this spring." The lead rider's tone was cool and lacked sincerity.

Frank recognized the rider addressing him as one of the sheriff's men, the one they called Cincinnati. "Thought I told you and your thugs to stay off of my land."

"Thugs?" Cincinnati feigned a hurt expression. "Well, that's not a very neighborly thing to say."

"You ain't my neighbor. You're just some asshole with a gun that some other asshole went and hung a badge on."

"You better not be callin' my pa no asshole you cripple son of a bitch." The comment came from a gaunt rider who was reaching for one of his two sidearms. Frank didn't know his name but had been confronted by him in the past.

"Now, Eli, I'm sure Mr. Gibson here didn't mean anything. We did come upon him quite sudden and unannounced. That's enough to put any man out of sorts," Cincinnati leaned forward in his saddle. "We've come here to do business not make threats."

"Them's one in the same as far as your sheriff's concerned."

"I'm sorry to hear you feel that way. I'm certain that Sheriff Cain would be anxious to dispel any misconceptions you have about his intentions." Cincinnati's smile widened. "The sheriff himself has sent us to make you a generous offer concerning our previous negotiations."

"Negotiations my ass. I ain't sellin' my land. I told you that the first time and I've told your son of a bitch, weasel of a junior deputy here twice this month." Frank spat on the ground in front of the hooves of Eli's horse.

Eli pulled both of his guns. "Come on, Cincinnati, let me kill him so we can get this over with."

"Keep those peacemakers holstered. I told you we are not here to threaten Mr. Gibson."

Eli opened his mouth to reply, but caught Cincinnati's glare and holstered his guns.

ABBY WAS INSIDE the stable when she heard the men's voices. She came outside to see four men on horses, two wearing badges.

"What the hell is goin' on here? Daddy, you alright?" Abby walked quickly to her father who stood facing the riders.

"I'm fine, Abigail." Frank waved her away. "Go on inside."

"Well, who might this exquisite creature be?" Cincinnati removed his hat. The steel of his ivory-handled colt reflected the low sunlight. "I, miss, am Sheriff's Deputy Cincinnati and these—"

"I don't give a shit who you are. Daddy said to get off our land and I expect you to do so." She stood to the cabin side of her father, her hands on her hips.

"Miss Gibson, might I say that it is uncommonly impolite for a woman such as yourself to speak in such a manner, let alone to interrupt a gentleman like myself." Cincinnati replaced his hat. "I only wish to make some pleasant introductions so as to further dispel any misconceptions you or your father may have toward the sheriff's department. Now, if you have no further objections, may I please continue?"

Caught off guard by the deputy's manner of speech, Abby failed to respond.

"Why, thank you. Now, I am Sheriff's Deputy Cincinnati, these men behind me are Victor Clay and Luther Jacoby. They work for Sheriff Cain's mining outfit." He jerked a thumb at the two riders directly behind him. One was lanky and strong looking but had a large pot belly that hung out over his belt. A Winchester with brass fittings was across his saddle. The younger one was short, hairy and dirty and wore a couple of old revolvers on his hips.

"And the gentleman to my right is Deputy Eli Cain." He made a sweeping gesture at Eli with his hand. "As I was telling your father, we are just your humble neighbors wishing to conclude some business."

"I still don't give a shit," Abby said. "Beggin' your forgiveness for my uncommonly impolite goddamn manner."

"I told you she was somethin' else, Cincinnati." Eli maneuvered his horse around until he was directly beside Abby. "Ain't no woman in these parts looks or acts like her. She's a real cherry." He leaned over the front of his saddle and slowly looked her up and down. He licked his lips like a dog anticipating a bone.

Abby felt she was being undressed by the deputy's leering eyes. She was about to reach for the Colts at her hips before realizing she wasn't wearing them. Now she felt doubly naked.

"You remember me, darlin'? You ready for what I got?" Eli put his hand in the front of his pants.

Clay and Jacoby laughed.

"Eli, I told you to keep your piece holstered," Cincinnati said, keeping his eyes on Frank. "So, Mr. Gibson. Are you ready to hear Sheriff Cain's offer?"

Frank returned the stare. "I ain't gonna sell."

"Well, now that's very disappointing." Cincinnati shook his head as his smile slowly disappeared. "By that answer I have to assume you are no longer interested in further negotiations and do not wish to hear sheriff Cain's proposal."

"That's about right."

"That's fair." Cincinnati sat back in his saddle. "I can accept and respect your position. Unfortunately, if I return to Sheriff Cain and inform him of your unwillingness to listen to his proposal, he will not be pleased with me or, I'm sorry to say, with you. So, in our mutual best interest, I must find a way to continue negotiations without you. Perhaps Miss Gibson here would be more open to our proposal. Eli, would you mind sequestering young miss - Abigail, was it? - and apprise her of our generous offer?"

"Goddamn right I can." Eli licked his lips again.

"And if you can't convince her, I'm sure Mr. Clay and Mr. Jacoby can." Cincinnati motioned to the two men behind him while keeping his gaze on Frank.

Clay and Jacoby eyed Abby and let out excited hoots.

Feeling helpless without her Colts, Abby took a step back. As she did so, she noticed sudden movement along the side of the cabin.

Beckett covered the distance between the cabin and the riders in a few quick strides before reaching Eli. Grabbing him by his gun belt, Beckett pulled him to the ground and stood over him, the Bowie placed tight against the deputy's throat. Eli let out a terrified screech, causing his horse to back up.

The surprise on Cincinnati's face gave way to growing anger.

Beckett leveled his gaze at the deputy. "You were asked to leave. I suggest you do so."

Eli slowly reached for one of his guns. Beckett crushed his hand with the heel of his boot. Eli let out another cry.

"Well, if it isn't our local mountain man." Cincinnati's mouth was drawn tight. "It seems you have quite the knack for attacking sheriff's deputies. That's not a healthy pastime, my friend."

"Told you I ain't your friend. Now, are you gonna leave or am I going to have to spill this worthless piece of shit, rapist's insides across the road?" Beckett pressed his blade against the skin of Eli's neck drawing a few beads of blood which trickled down to the dirt. Eli stopped squirming beneath Beckett's weight.

Composing himself Cincinnati waved off the anxious guns that Clay and Jacoby had drawn. "I have no quarrel with you, mountain man, though I cannot understand why you continue to interfere with sheriff's business."

"If you can't understand it, I ain't gonna explain it to you. Now, are you gonna leave?"

As Beckett stared Cincinnati down he was joined by a grey mutt who took its place beside him. The dog barked and growled, showing its teeth to the deputy.

"Fine, Mr. Beckett we'll leave. Just know that our business with Mr. Gibson and his lovely daughter has not been completed. We will be back when there aren't as many ..." Cincinnati glared at Beckett. "... complications."

Beckett removed his Bowie from Eli's neck and took his foot off of his hand.

Eli got to his feet and immediately went to his guns.

"Eli!" Cincinnati said. "It can wait."

Eli faced Beckett, his hands hovering over his guns. Beckett holstered his Bowie, staring at Eli then took a step closer.

"Eli!" The force of Cincinnati's voice stopped all motion. "Get on your horse."

Eli backed off and mounted his horse.

"I'm not done with you, mountain man." Eli turned his horse to leave.

As the three men headed west down the dirt road towards the trees, Cincinnati looked back at Beckett before following them.

"Oh, and you might want to keep your canine under control, Mr. Beckett. We wouldn't want to have to put him down now would we?" Cincinnati pointed at the dog and mimed a firing gun with his hand. The dog growled at him as he turned and rode off.

Before heading to the stable, Frank hobbled over to Beckett and placed his hand on his shoulder. "Thank you, son."

Beckett turned to Abby. "You okay?"

She smiled and looked at his holstered Bowie. "Now that's what I call intimidation."

TWELVE

"**WHAT THE HELL** was that about?" Beckett said, following Frank into the stable. Abby had gone into the cabin, assumably to put on her Colts. "Why didn't you tell me Cain was after your land?"

"Never came up I guess," Frank was wiping his tools off with a greasy rag and placing them into a wooden box.

"How long they been comin' down on you?"

"Not too long after the last time you were here. Didn't see it as a problem at first. Sheriff Cain himself came the first time. Well spoken fella. Kind of arrogant but most big city rich folk are I guess. Said he wanted to buy my station and I told him no. He accepted it and left. Wasn't 'til that Cincinnati fella started comin' round did they start gettin' pushy."

"No offense, Frank but why would they want your old way station anyway? Even the Fargo coach stopped comin' here after they built the railroad."

"That's just it. The railroad." Frank sat down on the same bail of hay Beckett had used to write on that morning. He leaned his gnarled cane against his knee. "Cain needs to get his gold to Chicago 'cause that's where his bankers are. That new railroad stretches all the way to Chicago but to get to it from these mountains and Cain's gold mines you gotta head seventy miles north over the pass to White Pine or backtrack eighty miles to Rathdrum. Lots of chances for a coach full of gold to get held up either direction."

"I still don't see what that has to do with your station."

Frank pointed to the west. "Ten miles down that road is Cain's mine." He turned and pointed south. "And ten miles down that road is Wallace. The Northern Pacific is busy cuttin' a spur from Missoula out this direction. Guess where it's gonna end up."

"Wallace." Beckett nodded his understanding.

"Next year Cain will have a twenty mile trip from his mine to the brand new train depot in Wallace and a straight shot to Chicago. Be rather convenient for them to have a way station smack in the middle to store animals, men and gear now wouldn't it?"

Beckett crossed his arms, leaned against a beam and looked up at the sky peeking through the boards in the ceiling.

"This is only gonna get worse. If them boys want this station that bad they're gonna take it."

"Yup. I know Abigail is good with them guns but, bless her heart, she ain't no killer. They really want to, they'll just come on in here and kill us - doin' who knows what to my darlin' daughter first - and that will be that." Frank looked up at Beckett. "Unless a fella who is capable of doin' what needs to be done stays around for a while. A fella who has done it before. A fella who has a soft spot for my Abigail."

Frank looked directly into Beckett's eyes.

"I see how she looks at you. I'm an old man, I ain't gonna be around forever. This wouldn't be a hard place for a fella like you to settle down would it?"

"I'm headin' south, Frank." Beckett hesitated a beat, then looked away. "It's time."

"Colorado," Frank said. It wasn't a question. "Well, I knew you'd have to sooner than later. I also know it ain't somethin' I can talk you out of."

"You can't."

The two men fell silent.

Frank broke the quiet, pulling himself up by his cane. "I've known you for a long time, Beckett. Other than Abigail, you're the only family I got. We'll get through this." He put his hand on Beckett's shoulder. "Worst case, I'll just sell to them bastards to save our necks. Maybe I'll go make nice with my wife."

Beckett smiled. "I know that's bullshit." After another beat he said, "I really wish I could help, Frank. I just—"

"I know, son." Frank patted his shoulder before heading toward the door.

THIRTEEN

"HAPPY BIRTHDAY, my friend," Doc Sherman placed a glass of gin on top of the piano. "Tonight we celebrate."

"Thanks, Doc." Nat was playing the piano to a full saloon.

Georgia Sherman sat on a stool next to Nat and whispered a song suggestion to him. She'd had a few drinks and was more playful than usual.

"Okay, Mrs. Sherman but only if you sing it,"

"Try and stop me." She stood up and leaned against the piano.

Nat's long fingers glided along the keys as he played her song. He nodded to her and she began to sing.

"Will you come with me my Phillis, dear, to yon blue mountain free ..."

Doc returned to the bar and filled a couple of empty glasses, placing one in front of Harvey Coleman who sat on the stool Beckett had occupied the day before.

"Hey, Doc. I wanna buy ol' Nat a drink too. Ain't no better piano player round these parts." Harvey lifted the glass in Nat's direction and took a long swig of beer.

"Will do Harvey." Doc pulled out a glass from below the bar.

"That mountain man friend of yours sure is somethin' ain't he?"

"Who, Beckett? Tell you the truth, before yesterday I'd never seen the son of a bitch swat a fly let alone take down a monster like Mord."

"Think he has any right tellin' us if'n we should take on the sheriff?"

"Don't know." Doc reached for a special bottle of gin he had hidden behind the bar. "But I think he might be right."

"What? You tellin' me you're gonna pull that ten-gauge off the wall and go after them assholes 'cross the street?"

"I ain't gonna do it myself but it might be something we all should consider." Doc filled the glass nearly full. "I ever tell you where I got that old ten-gauge, by the way?"

Harvey opened his mouth to answer but was unable to get out a word before Doc continued. "Doc Holiday gave me that coach shotgun when I was in Tombstone a few years back. Known him since medical school. We're old pals, you know. Anyway, that's the gun he shot that son of a bitch Tom McLaury with at the OK Corral. Gave it to me seeing as Georgia and I was heading up here and he wanted to make sure we was safe. Good man that Doc Holiday. Keep it loaded but ain't never used it. Kind of like you and that Walker Colt."

"Just because I don't pull this thing out every time them deputies are around doesn't mean I'm afraid to use it." Harvey placed his hand on the gun at his side.

"Sure, Harvey." Doc took the glass of gin over to the piano.

"... *Wait for the wagon, wait for the wagon and we'll take a ride* ..." Georgia held the final note as Nat finished playing and the miners in the room hooted and whistled their approval.

"That was wonderful, darling."

"Why, thank you, love." Georgia bent her husband over for a long kiss, forcing Doc to spill a portion of the drink he was carrying. The room erupted in hooting and whistling again. After releasing him from her embrace, she acknowledged the crowd with an exaggerated bow before moving through her adoring audience.

Doc composed himself and placed the second glass of gin on the piano next to the one already there. "Now let's hear Nat sing one."

Nat rapidly downed both glasses then slurred, "Anythin' you want to hear, Doc?"

"How 'bout Darlin' Nelly Gray?"

"You got it." Nat tickled the keys lightly and sang. "*Oh! My poor, Nelly Gray, They have taken you away and I'll never see my darlin' any more* ..."

Doc lingered by the piano, smiling as he surveyed the room. Georgia had made her way over to one of the poker tables and was giggling on the lap of one of Sherman Saloon's regulars. Others were laughing or talking loudly. He hadn't seen his customers this happy and carefree since before Cain and his men had moved into town.

As he relished the moment, the batwings flew open and three figures slipped in from the darkness outside. Sheriff

Cain and Deputy Mordecai led the way followed by Deputy Cincinnati.

Most of the patrons paused what they were doing to watch the three men take over a table in the far corner, Cincinnati sitting with his back to the corner while the other two faced him.

Oblivious to their arrival, Nat continued singing. *"... I'm a sittin' by the river and I'm weeping all the day ..."*

"GOD, I HATE IT when that nigger sings." Mordecai leaned forward in his chair, his elbows on the table.

As Cincinnati scanned the room from below his dark, flat-brimmed hat, Doc Sherman arrived with a bottle of whiskey and three glasses. "Sheriff Cain, Mordecai, Cincinnati." He nodded at each in turn then filled their glasses, placing the bottle on the table when finished. "A bit of your usual."

The lighthearted atmosphere that filled the room before slowly resumed as Doc recrossed the saloon to take his place behind the bar.

"You want to tell me exactly what happened out at old Frank Gibson's place?" Cain fingered his shot glass without drinking, leveling the question at Cincinnati.

"When I was finished ensuring that we were still on schedule at the mine, I headed out to Gibson's way station. Eli and a couple of his associates insisted on accompanying me. When we arrived I attempted to approach Gibson with your offer and he refused. It was at that point the mountain man called Beckett pulled Eli from his horse and threatened to kill him if we didn't leave."

"Mordecai here says this mountain man carries nothing but a knife. How did he get the upper hand on four armed men?" A small amount of liquid slopped over as Cain continued fiddling with his glass.

"After experiencing resistance from Gibson I tried to reason with his daughter when this maniac jumped Eli. I wanted to finish the deal to your satisfaction and I figured that killing the mountain man, an obvious acquaintance of Gibson, would hinder that outcome. I was also under the impression we needed to persuade this Beckett to sell us his claim. If you wish to take our negotiation tactics to the next level, I'd be happy to do so." Cincinnati placed his right hand on his ivory-handled Colt then picked up the glass in front of him with his left, holding it up in a salute to Cain before downing the contents.

In the background, the song continued. "... *for you've gone from the old Kentucky shore ...*"

"If that goddamned piano player don't stop singin' them goddamned songs I'm gonna end him." Mordecai gingerly touched his bandaged nose and looked back toward the piano.

Ignoring his son's comment, Cain responded to Cincinnati. "For now let's keep things on the up and up. Killing a drunk for pulling a gun on you in the street is one thing but killing men to take their land will just cause complications in the long run, complications I'd just as soon avoid now that our plans are back on schedule."

"That mountain man's a son of a bitch." Mordecai tore his attention away from the piano playing long enough to drain his glass. "Wish you'd let me blow his teeth out the back of his head. If he's still around while I'm running this town, things are going to be different."

"That's actually something I wanted to talk to you about, Mordecai." Cain refilled the glass in front of his son who downed it in one swift motion. "I've decided to take a different approach to that situation. With the reports the geologists have given me about sites two and three, it appears my mining operation here may be even bigger than the ones in California. I'm going to need to trust that the person I leave behind to run things won't blow his top every time some mountain man calls him a name."

"But, Pa, I ain't—"

"That is why I've wired your brother Zebediah. He and his men will be here in two days to head up the operation here in Temperance. You will accompany Cincinnati and me to the Black Hills to oversee our prospects there."

"I can handle it, Pa. I swear."

"Zebediah is a perfect choice for the job. He has the experience and the intelligence needed. He also may be the only gunman in the West who's faster than Cincinnati here."

The right side of Cincinnati's mouth curled up in a smirk.

Mordecai slumped back in his chair then slapped the table and grabbed the bottle of whiskey. He gulped nearly half before slamming the bottle down.

The piano player continued to sing. *"... the white man bound her with his chain, they have taken her to Georgia for to wear her life away ..."*

"That's fucking it." Mordecai rose from the table and pushed his way to the piano.

DOC LOOKED UP to see Mordecai standing over Nat. "Don't you know anything but them nigger songs?" Mordecai glared at Nat.

Nat stopped playing and looked up, his eyes hazy from the gin. He was about to stutter a response when the huge deputy grabbed him by the neck and threw him to the ground. Nat's skull bounced off the wooden floor with a hollow thud and his eyes rolled back.

Silence filled the saloon as Doc ran out from behind the bar, driven by an instinctive urge to help his friend.

"I don't like your voice and I don't like how your fingers play the piano." Mordecai lifted Nat up by his shirt. "I think we need to do somethin' 'bout that."

Cincinnati was about to get up when Sheriff Cain grabbed his arm.

Cain nodded at Mordecai. "Let him have this one. He needs it. No one's gonna miss a dead nigger."

Mordecai dragged Nat across the floor and out onto the wooden sidewalk in front of the saloon. Cain and Cincinnati followed along with everyone else.

"Reed," Mordecai said to a man standing in front of the bank."Get me some rope and some rawhide."

Nat lay limp in Mordecai's grasp. As he gradually regained his senses, his eyes widened in fear, looking up at the huge deputy.

"I've had it with you." Mordecai turned Nat around and bent him over the railing in front of Sherman Saloon.

Doc approached Sheriff Cain, desperation in his voice. "I don't know what he said to offend you but I'd be happy to make it up to you and your men."

Mordecai heard the plea. "Bein' a no good nigger's all he's done and there ain't nothin' you can do about it."

The man called Reed arrived with a length of rope and a strand of rawhide.

"Tie the rawhide 'round his pinkies." Mordecai had little trouble holding a wriggling Nat against the railing.

Reed looped the strand of rawhide below the knuckle of the little finger on each of Nat's hands. When he was done he attached the strand to the rope and yanked, stretching Nat's arms out, insuring the knots were solid.

"Throw the rope over that beam and attach it to your saddle." Mordecai leaned into Nat to keep him from falling.

"You can't do this." Doc looked around for help and caught Harvey Coleman's eye. He gestured at Harvey's revolver. Harvey answered by slinking back into the saloon.

Doc turned to Cain. "Sheriff, please stop this."

The sheriff didn't move.

When the rope was attached to the saddle horn and pulled tight, Reed nodded to Mordecai. As Mordecai steadied him, Nat's arms extended straight up, drawn taut by his pinkies being pulled up toward the beam above the sidewalk.

"This should make it harder to play those goddamn songs," Mordecai snarled into Nat's ear.

Mordecai unholstered his gun and pointed it into the air. He pulled the trigger. With the explosion the horse took off. The rope went taut for a brief moment. Then, with two quick pops, it disappeared into the darkness as Nat's scream penetrated the night.

After letting Nat fall to the ground, Mordecai grabbed the piano player by the wrists and showed everyone his hands. The pinkie of each hand was severed at the knuckle with white bone visible. Blood streamed from the stumps and poured down Nat's wrists onto Mordecai's hands.

"I'm done taking shit from you people. Let this be a lesson to all of you." Mordecai dropped Nat's hands and wiped blood onto Nat's pressed white shirt. He gave him one last kick in the gut before walking across the street.

Sheriff Cain and Cincinnati followed, stepping over the writhing piano player.

Doc was kneeling down to help his friend when he looked up to see two large metal barrels above him. Georgia stood pointing his ten-gauge shotgun at Mordecai. As she pulled the hammer back on the first barrel, an explosion twisted her body unnaturally and she fell against the front of the saloon. Another explosion pinned her to the wall where she slowly slumped down to the wooden sidewalk. A trail of blood followed her down the wall.

"Georgia!" Doc rushed to cradle his wife. Her body was limp and lifeless. Blood poured out of two huge holes in her chest. He looked over to Cincinnati who was reloading his smoking Colt.

"You've really got to keep your people under control." Cincinnati turned and continued walking to the bank.

Doc let out a cry as he held his wife. His friend moaned in agony in a pile next to him. The people of Temperance who'd made their way into the street with the commotion stood helpless watching Sheriff Cain and his men enter the bank.

FOURTEEN

ABBY SENSED that neither her father nor Beckett wanted to talk when they came in from the stable so she did't push it. Consequently, the three of them sat in silence throughout supper, the only sound in the cabin coming when a spoon periodically hit the side of a bowl as they ate stew.

When her father finished, he pushed himself away from the table, kissed her on the forehead and escaped to his room, leaving Abby and Beckett alone in the quiet.

After supper, Abby watched from the window as Beckett went outside. He slouched onto the wooden bench, poured himself a tin cup of whiskey then reached down to pet the grey mutt that sat at his feet.

A while later, Abby joined him, leaning on the railing in the same place as she had the night before. She noted the air wasn't as warm, a trace of fall crispness having arrived.

"Where'd that mutt come from anyway? Been lurking 'round here ever since I started cookin'."

"Been followin' me since I left my place. Slept in the stable with me last night. Was kinda leery of you. Guess he's over that now."

As though understanding what had just been said, the mutt stood up, walked across the porch and sat next to her, leaning against her leg. He lifted his head and directed imploring black eyes up at her. Unable to resist, she petted the dog's head. "I like him."

She reached into her skirt pocket and pulled out a piece of old rabbit meat she'd saved from the stew. The mutt sniffed her extended hand then delicately lapped up the offered treat. Wagging its tail, the dog nuzzled her more.

"Looks like you're his new favorite. Can't blame him really."

"You give him a name?"

"Nah, never was no good with that. Call my sorrel 'horse'."

"Well, I think he looks like a Baxter."

"Baxter?"

"Momma was seein' a fella named Baxter few years back. Real jackass, you ask me. Nice name though. Had a long beard was the same color as our friend here. Just looks like a Baxter is all." She reached down and again petted the grateful animal.

"Well, if you keep feedin' him I'm sure he'll stick 'roud here. Think he'll be just fine with you callin' him Baxter." He took a sip from the tin cup and appeared to relax after swallowing.

As she passed her hand over the mutt's wiry hair, Abby watched Beckett in the near darkness. The subtle glow through the window from the fire inside cast contrasting amber light and dark shadow on his face, making him look older. His strong sharp features and unreadable eyes reminded her of how her father looked when she was little.

"What were you writin' this morning? . . If 'n you don't mind me askin'."

Beckett hesitated before answering. "Was writin' a letter."

"To who?"

Beckett took another sip. "Was writin' a letter to my boy."

"Your boy?"

"My son."

"I didn't know you had a son."

"Didn't know Frank had a daughter and I've known him a lot longer than you've known me."

"Where is he?"

Beckett swirled the whiskey in his cup. "Colorado."

"That where you're headin' in the mornin'?"

"Got a few things to take care of first but, yes, that's where I'm headin'."

"You gonna send the letter off first? Tell him you're comin'?"

"Gonna deliver it myself. Got a envelope full of 'em"

Abby ruffled Baxter's ears then sat back, placing her hands on the railing. "You write to him regular?"

"More regular recently. First few years didn't write anythin'."

"Years? How long has it been since you seen him?"

"Ten years." Beckett finished his cup of whiskey.

"Why so long?"

He leaned forward, resting his elbows on his knees.
"Because he's dead."

FIFTEEN

"HELP ME GET HER onto the bar." Doc strained, pulling Georgia's body into the saloon. Harvey grabbed her legs and the two carried her across the room. Once placed on the bar, her arms fell off her chest and hung loosely on either side. Blood flowed in a steady stream onto the floor.

Doc opened her dress to examine the wounds. The first bullet had hit her in the liver. The second went straight through her heart.

"Doc, it's no use," Harvey said.

"Would someone get me my medical bag?"

"Doc, she's gone."

"Get me my goddamn medical bag!" Doc slammed his hand onto the bar.

Harvey took his arm and gently guided him away from the body. "Let her go." His voice was soft and calm.

Unable to take his eyes off his wife, Doc headed back to her side. Harvey grabbed him and turned him around so they were facing each other, forcing Doc to make eye contact. "Just let her go."

Doc tore away and returned to his wife's side where he gazed into her glossy, lifeless eyes, her face frozen in a look of shock.

"Doc," Harvey pleaded. "Nat needs you."

Doc paused then took a deep breath. When he let it out he appeared in control again. He placed his hand over Georgia's eyes and closed them.

He turned to Harvey, his voice steady. "Get me my medical bag."

* * *

AN HOUR LATER, Doc and Nat sat in the middle of the room with Harvey across from them. The piano player stared straight ahead through a cloud of laudanum, his hands cleaned and bandaged. Doc faced his own world of pain without any medicine.

The saloon was nearly full with miners and half the town-folk lining the walls. Georgia's body lay on the bar under a sheet someone had thoughtfully placed over her. No one said anything for a long time until Doc broke the silence.

"What are we going to do about Cain and his men?"

"Don't know what we can do," Harvey said. "No one here's a fighter."

"Buford, Amos, you two fought in the war." Doc gestured to a couple of men by the door. "Paul and Julius and half the town fought off Indians settling here. We're all fighters if we need to be. Even you Harvey."

"I think Doc is right," said a younger miner standing next to the bar. "If we don't stand up to these men, we'll end up losing everything. I've already lost my claim. Don't want to lose my family too."

"Is it really worth gettin' killed over?" The speaker stood against the wall across from the bar. "Ain't there already been enough of that. Once the gold's gone Cain and his men will leave."

"And what's that leave us?" Doc stood up. "We can't have a town without a livelihood. We were here long before Cain showed up. We built this town, we can't let him destroy it. He's already destroyed enough." He looked over to the cloaked body on the bar.

"If we're gonna fight Cain we're gonna need a plan. If we just go at them, Cincinnati will take half of us out before we cross the street." Seamus McCready, the town butcher, spoke in his thick Irish brogue. "We need a leader."

"How 'bout that Beckett fella?" Harvey looked up at Doc. "He's the only person 'round here who's stood up to them and survived. Did quite the number on ol' Mord's face too. Wasn't he comin' here before he headed back to his claim? He's more a part of this town than them Cain boys."

"He is coming back but I don't know if he's planning on staying." Doc gave his head a slight shake. "Got the idea he's leaving."

Harvey rose from his chair. "Well then, we gotta convince him." He looked at the faces around the room. "We gotta try at least."

Nat struggled to a standing position knocking over his chair in the process. Doc quickly reached over to steady him. With every eye in the saloon on him, the piano player fought off his drugged stupor to return their gaze.

"We gotta try."

SIXTEEN

"OH MY GOD." Abby left the railing and joined Beckett on the bench. "I'm so sorry. I didn't mean to—"

"It's alright." She was close enough to him that he could smell her sunshine-kissed hair.

"How did it happen? Was it like your wife?"

Beckett's response was slow and measured as he looked off in the distance. "No. She died when he was only a year old. I raised him on our farm until he was seven and I was forced to sell our land. After that I took a job with a cattle outfit. It was hard on him livin' with them cowboys but I had no other way to make money. I chased them cows all over Nebraska, Kansas and Colorado, my boy in tow." He let out a deep sigh as though having just been relieved of a terrible burden.

"You raised him all by yourself?"

"Didn't have no other choice. He had a hard life, not much food, not much for a young boy to do."

"Why is it you got to go to Colorado to see him?"

"When he was about ten years old we was drivin' cattle past a town in Colorado called Durango. One day our boss gave us a few hours off so us cowboys went into town. I took Daniel, told him to keep out of trouble and went drinkin'."

Beckett paused. Grass on the valley floor was faintly visible in the starlight, swaying in the evening breeze.

"That night a gunfight broke out in a saloon. A man emptied his ivory-handled Colt into five men. His last bullet killed Daniel. I'd been so passed out drunk I didn't even find out 'till the next morning."

"My god." Abby lightly touched his arm.

"Buried him on a hill covered with dandelions there in Durango. He loved dandelions. I'm goin' there to deliver my letters to him."

He turned to see green eyes full of concern, looking at him.

"Anyway, that's who I was writing to this morning."

"You gonna track this man down, the man who shot him?"

"Ain't gonna bring my boy back."

Abby took her hand away from his arm and turned to face the tree line.

Several minutes passed before she broke the silence. "You gonna stay down there in Durango or you gonna come back here?"

"I would if'n I had something to come back to."

She turned back to him, her green eyes peering into his, a slight furrow on her brow. Placing her soft hands on either side of his face, she drew him close then gave him a long deep kiss.

Though he had dreamt of such a moment since he first saw her, Beckett was the first to break the embrace. With a trace of a smile on his face, he stood. "I think I'd better turn in."

"You don't have to ..." She hesitated, uncertainty in her voice. "... sleep in the stable I mean."

"Unfortunately, I do." He walked off the porch, but turned as he reached the last step. "I'll see you in the morning, Abby."

Beckett took large strides into the darkness back to the stable, sensing her eyes on him all the way.

"Good night, Beckett," she called out as he went inside the stable.

* * *

THE NEXT MORNING Beckett woke to the sound of a pair of sparrows serenading each other. He sat up and stretched out his sore arm, the pain of the bear's bite still with him. He looked down at his soiled and tattered long underwear and decided to remove them. A fresh pair would be waiting for him when he picked up his list of supplies from Jasper's store. After dressing and packing up his horse, he went to the cabin.

Abby was preparing eggs in a skillet over hot coals. Frank sat in his rocker looking out the open door toward the western tree line.

"You all ready to head out?" Frank held a cup of coffee in his hand.

"Thanks for letting me stay, Frank."

"Only wish it could have been longer." The old man took a sip and placed the cup on the table.

"You gonna have breakfast?" Abby looked up from her cooking, her face aglow from the warmth of the fire.

"Thanks but I'd better get on the road. Leavin' my mule here. Ain't got no use for him now." He walked over to Frank and offered his hand. "I've decided to take care of your problem. I won't let them harass you anymore."

Frank struggled to his feet and clasped the extended hand. "You don't have to do that, Beckett."

"Yes I do."

After shaking hands, Beckett turned to Abby, meeting her green eyes. They held the gaze for a long moment before he tipped his hat to her and walked out the door. Mounting his sorrel, he rode north towards Temperance. Baxter the mutt sat on the porch, his ears alert, watching Beckett leave.

SEVENTEEN

SAMUEL BAINES SAT on the bank of the creek that flowed behind his parents' shop on Main Street. The brand new outfit his mother had laid out for him that morning was already soiled with grass and mud. He held a long pole made from a willow branch. Attached to its tip was a line that cut through the slow moving water. He had been lulled into a trance by the noises from the woods and the warmth of the late morning sun when movement on the water broke the spell. A dragonfly landed on the water three feet from his line. It floated on the surface until it disappeared with a sudden splash into the mouth of a large trout. He stood in an effort to catch a glimpse of the colorful fish diving beneath the water, wondering why it hadn't gone for his worm.

"Just missed that one." The voice came from behind him.

"Mr. Beckett!" Samuel turned so quickly he yanked the pole with him. "You *did* come back."

"I told you I'd tell you if I was leavin'."

"Wanna help me catch that big rainbow?"

"Think we'd have a better chance if your worm wasn't trying to escape by foot."

Samuel returned his attention to his line only to find the end of it on the edge of the creek near the bank with the worm wiggling in the mud.

"Oops." He took a step forward, lifting his pole at the same time, then dropped the line back in the water.

Beckett ruffled his mop of hair then sat down onto the bank next to him, placing his saddlebag to the side on the soft grass.

Samuel joined him, resuming the relaxed posture he'd had before the trout took the dragonfly. He checked his line then stirred dirt on the bank with his shoe. "You get all your errands taken care of?"

"Almost."

"You missed a good supper. Ma made pork chops and gravy. Got 'em on special at the butcher."

"Sorry I missed it. I love pork chops."

"Pa's got your list ready for you. I helped him collect it."

"Good. I'll have to pick it up when we're done here."

Samuel looked at Beckett out of the corner of his eye. The mountain man was large, strong and appeared fearless. Samuel tried to emulate him by sitting erect and puffing out his chest, but was unable to hold the position.

"Had some bad stuff happen here last night," Samuel said.

"What kind of bad stuff?"

"A situation down at the saloon. Deputies hurt the black piano player ..." Samuel paused. "And killed Mrs. Sherman."

"What do you mean they killed Mrs. Sherman?" Beckett turned, putting his hand on Samuel's shoulder. "What deputies?"

"Mordecai did something bad to Nat and when Mrs. Sherman went after him, Cincinnati shot her. I wasn't there but I heard about it down at the livery this morning."

Beckett stood. "Georgia Sherman is dead?"

"That's what I heard."

The mountain man looked in the direction of the sheriff's office his jaw clinched. He was silent for a minute before kneeling.

"Listen, Samuel. I want you to promise me that no matter what happens while I'm in town, you stay inside your parents' store. I have a feeling that these bad men are only gonna get worse. You gotta promise me."

"I promise." Samuel crossed his heart. "You gonna stop them?"

"Gonna try."

Beckett picked up his saddlebag, threw it over his shoulder and walked along the bank of the creek behind the buildings on Main Street.

"Mr. Beckett," Samuel called after him. "If Cincinnati really is Duke Valentine, he's a cold-blooded killer like no other. You sure that Bowie is gonna be enough?"

Beckett just kept walking.

EIGHTEEN

WHEN BECKETT reached the alley next to Sherman Saloon, he took a glance toward the jail making sure to keep in the shadow of the building. Cincinnati was standing in the exact position he'd been when Beckett had first seen him, leaning up against the post with his thumb behind his belt buckle. The large red jewel on his tie sparkled in the sunlight. Six horses were tied in front of Cain's bank next door but there were no riders in sight.

As Beckett reached the saloon's back door he was almost knocked backwards when it swung outward.

Harvey Coleman looked startled when he recognized who stood in his way.

"Beckett. You're here. I was just headin' out to look for you."

"You're lookin' for me?"

"Sure. We all are." Harvey reversed direction and held the door open for Beckett to follow.

As they entered the saloon, Harvey announced, "Found him."

The front door was latched and curtains covered the windows, keeping daylight from entering. Candlelight from wall sconces and the large chandelier overhead enhanced the somber atmosphere in the room.

Five men sat in an imperfect circle around Doc whose chair was in the middle of the saloon. Next to him slouched the piano player, his hands bandaged with bright red showing through where his little fingers should have been. The thin black man was listless, staring straight ahead at the back wall, his dead-to-the-world bearing in sharp contrast to the effervescent personality Beckett had met two days earlier.

Harvey walked behind the bar, poured himself a shot of whiskey and downed it then refilled the glass.

Doc looked up at Beckett, emptiness registering in his eyes.

"Beckett. I'm glad you're here." Doc's voice was weak and cracked, making him sound like a person recovering from laryngitis. "Harvey, can you pour Beckett a glass of that English ale?"

Harvey took a glass from beneath the bar and filled it from the barrel on the counter. He slid the glass over to Beckett, slopping some of the foamy head over the side as it stopped.

Beckett nodded to Doc as he took a sip even though he wasn't in the mood for a drink. He turned back to Harvey and spoke in a low voice only the miner could hear. "What happened here last night?"

Harvey grabbed a rag and wiped up the excess ale on the bar next to Beckett. Keeping his voice equally low, he said, "Nat here was playin' and singin' like he does and for some reason that asshole Mordecai took offense to him. He then proceeded to throw Nat to the ground and pulled him out to the front, tied his pinkies to a horse and tore 'em clean off. Blood was everywhere. Then, Georgia bein' as feisty as she is, raised Doc's ten-gauge at Mord and Cincinnati shot her twice in the chest. She died right there in the front of the saloon."

Beckett leaned against the bar taking it in.

"How's Doc handlin' it?"

"He ain't as good as he's pretendin'. Casket maker came and took Georgia's body this mornin'. She was lyin' here on the bar all night." Finished with his wiping, Harvey drained a second shot of whiskey. "Poor Nat's been sittin' in a laudanum stupor since Doc bandaged him up."

Beckett put down his glass of ale without taking another drink and placed his saddlebag on the bar before sitting across from Doc and Nat. Leaning forward he said, "I'm so sorry about Georgia, Doc. She was a special woman."

Doc acknowledged Beckett's sentiments with a slight nod. "Think most folks here thought that way. Shouldn't have happened to her."

Nat moved in his chair, apparently coming out of his haze. "She shouldn't have gone after 'em. Not on account of me."

"You didn't do nothin' to them boys," Harvey said from behind the bar. "That Mord's just a maniac. You and Georgia both didn't deserve what they done to you."

Beckett turned his attention to Nat. "How you holdin' up?"

Nat held up his bandaged hands. "Guess that big deputy ain't gonna have to put up with my songs no more."

"Why's that?" Beckett reached out and took hold of Nat's wrists, holding up his damaged hands. "I ain't no musician but once they heal, I count eight good piano playin' fingers. Can't let a man like that get his way just 'cause he's evil."

"Well, Beckett, we've all been talkin' 'bout that." Harvey came around from behind the bar and stood next to Nat. "We heard what you was sayin' when you was here last and we're ready to stand up to Cain and his men."

"Good. That's the only way this town's gonna get out from under his boot."

"Exactly." Doc's voice was clearer, almost normal. "That's why we want you to help us take him down."

"Me?" Beckett leaned back in his chair.

"An army is only as good as its leader," Seamus McCready said. "From what we've seen you're the best we got."

Beckett shook his head. "I ain't no leader."

"And we ain't no army," Doc said. "We're just gonna have to figure it out."

Everyone in the room had their eyes on Beckett.

"Listen, fellas, I got my own plans for Cain. I ain't got room for yours too."

"Who says our plans ain't the same?" Doc's voice was back to full force.

"I do." Beckett stood. "If you want Cain to stop runnin' you off your land and takin' your money, you tell him. Then, when he won't listen, you show him. I can't be a part of it."

"But you're just as much a part of this town as the rest of us," Harvey said. "What happens when Cain comes after your claim?"

"Ain't my claim no more. Sold it to Doc."

Harvey looked at Doc.

"It's true. My boys are already up there makin' plans." Doc paused, his voice breaking up again. "Don't even know about their mother yet."

Beckett placed his hand on Doc's shoulder while looking around the room. "This ain't my fight, fellas. Got one of my own and I aim to get to it."

With that, Beckett grabbed his saddlebag from the bar and slipped out the back door.

NINETEEN

AS BECKETT ROUNDED the back of Sherman Saloon he stopped, thinking about the plight of the men inside. For a second he considered returning and offering to make their fight his own. Then he thought about Frank, the man who was the closest thing to a real father Beckett had. Frank was also a friend, a man who truly knew Beckett yet still cared for him despite his imperfections. Now that friend and his daughter, whom he also cared for, were in mortal danger. To protect them he had to convince Cain and his men to abandon any hopes of acquiring Frank's land.

With renewed resolve he peered from behind the saloon and down Williams Street. A man from inside the bank came over to Cincinnati who still leaned against a post outside the jail. After a brief exchange, the deputy followed the man back into the bank.

Beckett detected no movement on the ground floor of the building through the main window to the right of the bank door, but saw considerable activity through the two second-floor windows. Outside of six shuffling horses tied in front of the bank and a dusty brown cat cleaning itself in front of the Main Street Hotel, the street was empty.

He walked across the dusty street, avoiding the deep wagon ruts while keeping an eye peeled in all directions. Stepping onto the boardwalk in front of the bank, he placed his back against the front wall and peered in through the large, barred window. The room was empty except for a teller and a guard who dozed on a corner stool, a shotgun cradled in one arm.

He continued down the boardwalk to the jail stopping just short of the entrance. The jail's only window was on the far side of the open door so he stood quietly for nearly a minute, listening for movement. Hearing none, he stepped onto the threshold.

The office area was small, containing a large desk on the left side of the room and two chairs. A rack full of Winchesters and a couple of shotguns hung on the wall behind the desk. A chain ran through the trigger guards of each weapon with the ends secured by a large padlock. There was nothing on the desk and no wanted posters lined the walls. At the back of the office was a doorway leading to four cells paired two a side.

To his right, Beckett could see the sleeping guard through an open entryway that connected the jail to the lobby of the bank. Taking a step inside the jail's entrance brought him in view of the teller behind his window handling something on a desk and to the far right, at the far end of the lobby, was the stairway to the second floor.

Beckett walked into the bank, past the sleeping guard, who was now drooling on his shirt, and up to the teller's window.

The teller looked up from the solitaire game he was playing, noticed Beckett, and quickly pushed his cards aside. Straightening his wire frame glasses, he approached the window. "Yes sir, how may I help you?"

Beckett glanced at the guard. "I'm lookin' for Sheriff Cain."

"Oh, the sheriff is in a meeting and cannot be disturbed. Is there anything I can do for you? Leave a message maybe."

"How 'bout Cincinnati and Mordecai? They up there too?"

"Deputy Cincinnati and Deputy Mordecai are attending the meeting also. I'd be happy to—"

"Thanks."

Beckett turned and walked past the now snoring guard, back into the jail. Instead of going out the front entrance, he went down the back hallway between the cells on either side of the hall. All four were empty and looked as if they'd never been used. At the back of the jail was a reinforced, metal door leading to the alley behind. Beckett opened the door and turned toward the rear of the bank.

On the backside of the bank was a second set of stairs going up to a door on the second floor. Being careful not to make a sound, he climbed the steps and stood on the landing with his ear against the door. He heard mens' voices but could not make out any words.

He reached up, took hold of the top of the building and pulled himself up until his elbows were locked, his waist touching the top. Throwing his right boot over he straddled the outside wall. The roof of the bank was flat, set two feet below the outside frame of the walls. In the four corners were square cutouts meant for drainage.

Not wanting to create any sound below by walking on the roof, Beckett stood up onto the outside wall, balanced himself on the narrow woodwork and edged his way toward the south side of the building next to the single-story post office. He didn't look down at the dusty ground thirty feet below but concentrated on placing one foot in front of the other.

There were two small windows on the south side of the bank facing the post office, the first about four feet in from the corner of the building. He stopped there and straddled the outer wall. Already he heard the voices inside more clearly.

He brought his leg over the wall and placed both feet on the roof. Taking off his hat, he placed it and his saddle-bag on the wall then grabbed the wall between his legs with both hands. He leaned backwards slowly, releasing his hands one at a time until he hung upside down on the side of the building, his weight supported by the backs of his knees. His head was only a couple of inches above the small window. He could hear the conversation inside perfectly.

TWENTY

CINCINNATI LEANED AGAINST the south wall of Sheriff Cain's office next to a small window, his arms crossed, keeping an eye on the stairwell to the lobby below. His presence wasn't really necessary. However, when Sheriff Cain summoned, you came. So when a miner named Finley fetched him with a message from Cain, he followed. Besides, it was just as easy to hold up the bank wall as it was the post in front of the jail.

The meeting opened with the foremen of the mines at sites one and two giving a status report. Periodically, Mordecai, who sat in one of the chairs in front of the sheriff's desk, interrupted with questions or observations meant to show he knew what was going on at each operation. Each time Sheriff Cain let him speak, but it was apparent by his demeanor he was uninterested in Mordecai's comments and eager for the foremen to continue.

Next followed the planning strategy for this afternoon's ore transport. Four hired gunmen from Seattle that Cincinnati had never met stood against the far wall trying to look tough.

"Deputy Eli has promised me that the shipment will be loaded up into four wagons by the time you men arrive there this afternoon." Cain leaned forward, putting his arms on his desk. He looked at Cincinnati. "How accurate is this information, deputy?"

"Eli and his boys already had two of the wagons loaded and locked down when I left yesterday. He should have ample time to get the other two wagons ready to go. Assuming he doesn't botch the job.

"That's a big assumption." Mordecai slumped back, a smirk on his face.

"I want one man on each wagon not including the driver and shotgun" Cain nodded toward the four men against the wall. "That's three armed men per wagon. Mordecai will take the lead and Cincinnati will take up the rear. Do you think Eli and a few of his men should accompany you, deputy?"

Cincinnati casually surveyed the men in the room. "No, sir. Fourteen men should be more than enough."

"Okay. After you get through the mountains, it's a relatively straight shot to the lake. You'll be in the trees almost the whole way so you'll need to stay alert. There are plenty of places for an ambush. Any questions?"

One of the Seattle men stepped forward to address Cain, shaking his head. "We can handle ourselves, sir. This is what we do."

"Once you reach Lake Coeur d'Alene there will be a steamer waiting for you to take you to Fort Sherman. Mordecai and Cincinnati have ridden the route and know exactly where to meet the steamer. When the wagons and their payloads are safely on the boat, you men are done. Return here and you'll get paid. Only my deputies and the drivers will accompany the wagons to the fort. From there I've arranged for a cavalry escort the rest of the way to the train depot in Rathdrum.

"Why not just take the pass north to White Pine?" one of the other Seattle men said.

"We've tried that with smaller shipments. Too much elevation, too many switchbacks. Overall it's too dangerous. I've managed to work out an arrangement with Fort Sherman for the use of a steamer but it's a one time deal. That's why we have such a large payload. We've been saving it up for the safer route. Once the spur to Wallace is completed, we'll have a straight, twenty-mile shot to a train depot. But, that won't happen until next year. This payload needs to go now."

Cain stood and walked around the room. His pace was slow, his hands clasped behind him like a drill sergeant. "This shipment is very important. That's why I'm paying you men so well for your services. I will not tolerate failure. Are we all clear?"

There were uniform nods from the men.

"Alright then, time's wasting. Get down to the mine and I'll see you back here when your job is complete. "

As everyone moved to leave, Cain added. "Cincinnati, hang back for a moment?"

Joining Cincinnati next to the small window, he watched until Mordecai and the four Seattle men were clear of the stairway.

"Deputy, even though I've given Mordecai the task to lead this transport, I don't need to tell you that you're the one in charge of this operation. I'm expecting you to make sure everything goes smoothly."

Cincinnati gave a slight nod. "I wouldn't have it any other way."

Cain moved closer, his tone confidential. "What I didn't tell the others is that this shipment isn't just ore. A month back we hit a vein and pulled out a huge amount of solid gold. There's over a quarter million in those four wagons."

Cincinnati's eyes widened as he pushed away from the wall.

"If we don't get this gold to the train and on its way to my investors in Chicago, the funding for the new spur will fall through. I don't care how lucrative the other sites are, if we can't safely get gold out of these mountains—"

"Don't worry, Sheriff. I'll get it there."

"I know you will." Cain placed a hand on Cincinnati's shoulder. "Because if you don't …" the grip tightened, "… you're the one I'll blame."

Cincinnati looked directly into the sheriff's eyes and nodded.

Cain released his hand. "Now, what are we going to do about this Beckett and his claim below site three? We need that claim, deputy, and at this point, I don't care how you get it."

"As soon as we return from the train …" Cincinnati paused at the top of the stairs, placing his hand on his smooth, ivory-handled Colt, "… I'll take care of the mountain man."

TWENTY-ONE

BECKETT'S FACE WAS FLUSH from the blood running to his head. He used his abdominal muscles to rise up far enough until he was able to grab the top of the building between his legs then pulled himself up the rest of the way into a sitting position. After putting his hat back on and throwing his saddlebag over his shoulder, he looked west down Main Street to see five riders kicking up dust as they rode out of town. He stretched out his lower legs to get the blood flowing again and waited until Cincinnati followed them then stood up on the narrow wall of the building and carefully retraced his steps to the landing and the stairs.

Once clear of the bank, he hurried along the rear of the buildings lining Main Street until he reached the creek behind the general store. Samuel was gone but Beckett's sorrel was still tied out back where he'd left it. He went to the horse and unhooked the rawhide drawstring that held the teardrop bag which held his provisions.

He circled the building to the front and entered the store. "Howdy, Lilly." Beckett tipped his hat to Samuel's mother standing behind the counter then nodded to her husband next to her. "Jasper."

"Well, Mr. Beckett, you back for your goods?" Jasper Baines said.

"I am but I'm in a bit of a hurry."

"No problem, I've got them all bagged up for you." Jasper reached down and lifted up a paper sack from behind the counter."

Beckett set his provisions bag on the counter, loosening the rawhide drawstring to open the top before transferring his supplies from the paper sack.

"So, you ain't stickin' 'round then," Jasper said.

"Not this time." Beckett finished filling the teardrop-shaped bag and drew the top tight.

"Samuel will be so disappointed," Lilly said.

Beckett glanced around the store. "Were is the boy?"

Jasper looked up at the ceiling for a second. "Oh, he's upstairs. Said he wasn't feeling good and wanted to stay inside and read."

Remembering his instructions to the boy to stay inside, Beckett smiled. "Well, tell him I said goodbye, would you?"

"Sure, Mr. Beckett."

Beckett slung the bag over his shoulder and was about to turn to leave before hesitating. "And could you tell him that I've gotta be movin' on? Won't be back here for quite a while. Wish'n I could tell him myself."

"He's right upstairs if'n you want to see him."

"Ain't got time." Beckett tipped his hat again to Lilly. "Thanks for the supplies."

"Hope to see you again, Mr. Beckett." Lilly smiled at him as she moved from behind the counter.

"Me too."

Beckett was nearly out the door when Jasper said, "Oh, wait." He walked over to a back shelf and returned with a jar full of a cherry colored liquid. "Totally forgot your lamp oil. Didn't come in until this morning. Forgot to put it in your bag."

As he gave it to Beckett with his left hand he hit his forehead with the heal of his right. He went to the register, opened it and took out a few coins. "And here's what was left over from your gold."

"Give it to Samuel. Tell him to get himself a new dime novel." Beckett turned and left.

* * *

THE TRAIL to the mine was well-traveled, weaving in and out of the thick ponderosa pines that lined the banks of the Coeur d'Alene River. After following Cincinnati and his men for two hours at a safe distance, Beckett rode into a small clearing surrounded by a grove of birch trees that rustled with the breeze. A woodpecker he'd heard for quite a distance, stopped its drumming, extended its large wings and soared low through the trees giving out a loud call.

In the center of the clearing was a circle of large river rock with the remnants of many campfires inside. The area immediately surrounding the circle of rock had once been nothing but packed earth created by significant boot traffic. Now the grass that carpeted the edge of the clearing was reclaiming its original domain. Rusty cans, bottles and other trash were strewn around the perimeter.

As he approached a large hill an hour later, a muted explosion echoed through the trees. Coming closer he heard sounds of men hitting rock with metal tools. While the trail veered to the east side of the hill, trees had been cleared creating a path to the river on the west, making the Coeur d'Alene fully visible. Though the river was wide at this point, it also appeared to be shallow with gently sloping banks on either side, the perfect place for fording.

The trail widened and rose in elevation as Beckett rode around the east side of the hill. At the top of the rise, rock had been blasted away, creating a cliff that fell straight down to a small stream fifty feet below. Cresting the rise, he stopped. The trail continued down and around, ending at the mining camp at the southern base of the hill.

Turning his sorrel, he followed the trail back to the north side of the hill then headed west, crossing the Coeur d'Alene. Once on the other side, instead of continuing on toward the lake, he rode south into the trees paralleling the river.

A few minutes later he passed a small cemetery tucked into the pines with an abandoned mine just five yards away. A thick layer of pine needles blanketed wooden headstones marking where miners were buried. Beckett took note of a shovel lying among the needles next to a large empty grave.

The camp near the mine consisted of a pair of dilapidated tents that had fallen against the rocks and an old outhouse that leaned against a large pine. No one had been there in a very long time.

Beckett dismounted and tied his horse to a tree. Opening his saddlebag, he removed the envelope full of letters, folded it, then carefully put it in his rear pants pocket. After reaching into his leather tear-shaped pouch and removing a box of matches, he untied his hatchet from its place on the saddle and slid it under his belt.

He retraced the route he'd just taken but this time on foot. After recrossing the river, he climbed the large hill from the north. When he reached the top, he stopped, crouching behind a pine. His damp pants clung to his thighs but were no longer dripping and were already beginning to dry.

The mining camp was situated in a large horseshoe-shaped recess at the base of the hill with the open end facing out. The trail Beckett had followed earlier entered the camp on the left after curling around the hill. Another trail exited the camp heading due east in the direction of Frank's place. The entrance to the mine was at the back of the horseshoe framed in railroad ties. The right side of the horseshoe was lined with canvas tents and small wooden buildings. Across from them stood a solid structure made of stacked railroad ties that could easily house four wagons. At the front were two large doors with locks and chains securing them. Two shotgun guards stood outside.

A small rail system led from the depths of the mine to a terminus in the center of the camp where a couple of empty mining carts sat. Cincinnati leaned against one of them, his thumbs behind his belt buckle, talking with Mordecai who looked irritated. Four men, presumably the gunmen from Seattle, sat on horses beside the large locked building.

Beckett scanned the camp. Toward the back of the horseshoe, away from the tents next to the large building was a raised platform with a canvas roof. Visible inside were stacks of wooden crates with the words "Danger High Explosive" stenciled across them next to a pile of large cans. A miner preoccupied with reading a newspaper stood beside the array.

The thick trees provided perfect cover as Beckett walked in a crouch toward the rear of the canvas tents. Keeping his eye on Cincinnati all the way, he bumped into a miner relieving himself on the rock wall.

"What the—"

Beckett grabbed the miner from behind, clamping a large hand over his mouth before he could say any more. The miner struggled for a moment until Beckett bounced his head off of the rock.

Beckett carefully placed the limp body on the ground and whispered, "Sorry about the headache."

Once he reached the edge of the tents, he was in the process of figuring a way to cross the rest of the horseshoe without being seen by Cincinnati and his men when a huge explosion rocked the ground and a large plume of dust bellowed from the open mine. As the deputies and their men covered their eyes with their hats, Beckett sprinted across the open space, through the wall of dust, and slid behind the stack of wooden crates on the platform.

Men came stumbling and coughing from the mine covered in dust. The entire camp ran to examine the damage including the man standing above Beckett with the newspaper.

"What happened?" Cincinnati said to one of the men from the mine.

"Don't know," he coughed. "We were about to blast. Something must have gone wrong."

"Well, get your men out of there. Shut down the mine if you have to. We don't have time to sort it out right now."

Taking advantage of the pandaemonium, Beckett surveyed the supplies on the platform. Next to the crates were large metal cans that read:

E.I. Dupont & Co. Black Blasting Powder 25 LBS

He picked up a can to feel its heft then slid his Bowie under the lid of one of the crates and pried it open. Inside were large sticks rolled in paper.

"Perfect."

TWENTY-TWO

CINCINNATI WATCHED as two miners pushed a tram along the rails from the opening until they stopped at the terminus beside him. They then began unloading its contents - four partial human bodies, the last one missing its lower half. Turning from the carnage, he walked to the large locked stable.

"We ready to go?"

The shotgun guard to whom he addressed his question had his eyes glued on the grisly scene in front of him and didn't respond immediately. "Think so. Eli's just doing the last check."

"Don't you think that right about now might be an appropriate time to open the doors and begin to get everyone in position?"

The guard snapped his attention to Cincinnati as he fumbled in his vest for his key. "Yes, sir." After unlocking the padlock holding the chain, he motioned to the other guard and the two swung the huge doors open.

Inside four covered wagons stood side by side, packed to the top with large crates. Cincinnati was marveling at the amount of gold and ore in the crates when Mordecai came up behind him.

"Ah, Mordecai. Could you please grab a few men and get the horses hitched to the wagons? We are running behind."

"But, I—"

"Horses. Wagons. Now." Cincinnati's tone was curt and harsh.

Mordecai lumbered over to a couple of horses tied in front of the stable. After unhitching them, he yanked their reins so hard one of the horses nearly stumbled to its knees before recovering.

Once the caravan was loaded and the men were positioned, Cincinnati gave the order to move out. Mordecai took the lead on his large draft horse. The four wagons followed, each carrying a driver armed with a pistol and a man riding shotgun holding a twelve-gauge. Behind each wagon rode one of the Seattle gunmen. The single-file procession moved along the trail back around the hill.

As Cincinnati mounted and started following the last wagon, Eli ran alongside. His eyes were sunk into his face, his cheekbones poking out below them. He had tried dressing like his father, but without the resources to afford his father's wardrobe, the result was a pathetic imitation. "Why can't I go with you fellas? I'm just as good with a gun as them Seattle boys and I got two of 'em."

"Eli, I need you here to help Clay and Jacoby sort out the mine explosion." Eli was about to protest when he added, "Listen, you did a fine job getting the shipment ready to go but I need you here. We have plenty of men for the job."

Eli's shoulders slumped as he walked back toward the mine.

Cincinnati shook his head as he gently kicked his mount in the ribs to catch up with the caravan. As he rode, he kept his senses alert. A blanket of clouds had recently covered the sky though the heat remained. Without the sun, the hard shadows of the pines below the hill were now a washed-out grey. The only sounds he heard were the hooves of the horses on the rocks.

As the first wagon crested the hill where they had blasted the rock wall earlier that year, Cincinnati spotted movement out of the corner of his eye. Scanning up the side of the hill, he detected a dark outline of a man crouching in the muted shadows of a group of large pines. As he pulled his Colt, he heard a faint, high-pitched hiss.

Immediately recognizing the sound, he yelled ahead, "Everyone move. It's an—"

Before he could finish, the side of the hill above the crest of the trail disappeared in an explosion of sound and light. The concussion was so powerful Cincinnati had to grab his saddle horn with both hands to keep from being knocked off his horse.

Up ahead the second and third wagons in the line were no longer on the trail, but were falling fifty feet to the stream below, spilling their riders into the air on the way. The trail, too, was gone, having been turned to rubble, creating a rain of dirt and rocks which accompanied the wagons in their fall. Mordecai and the first wagon sat safely on the other side of the new gap in the hill.

Cincinnati searched the rise for the figure he'd seen before, but instead glimpsed a small lighted object, sizzling as it fell toward the wagon in front of him. As he reined hard on his horse in a desperate attempt to back away, the object hit the roof of the wagon and slid down the canvas to the trail.

The explosion that followed disintegrated the wagon, sending bits of rock and wood in all directions. Cincinnati's horse reared and threw him onto the hard ground. The men who had been on the wagon, having jumped when they saw the first explosion were covered in debris in the bushes below the trail. The last Seattle gunman was less fortunate. After his horse bucked him off, the animal reared again, landing his hoof square on the gunman's temple.

Disoriented from the last concussion, his ears ringing, Cincinnati struggled to his feet. As he hurried up the trail, he saw the figure in the trees heading up the hill. Concentrating on keeping his hand from shaking, he aimed his Colt, cocked the hammer and pulled the trigger.

BECKETT'S EARS were sore from the explosions. With no previous experience with blasting powder, he was surprised when he not only destroyed the trail and three wagons, but also half the hill, not to mention killing as many as nine men.

As he ran up the hill through the trees he turned to look behind him. He saw Cincinnati fire but was powerless to keep from being hit. The bullet splintered the bark of a tree before burrowing into his left shoulder. He felt the sting before he heard the gunshot. A deep red patch began growing on his shirt as pain from the wound burned from the inside. He shook off the discomfort as he raced to intercept the lead wagon before it crossed the river.

Dodging trees all the way, Beckett ran at full speed down the opposite side of the hill. He found a hiding spot on the north side of the hill just before the trail veered toward Temperance. Crouching behind a tree on a steep slope that looked down on the trail ten feet below, he checked to make sure his Bowie was in its holster and his hatchet was still stuck behind his belt just as Mordecai headed down the trail at a fast trot ahead of the remaining wagon.

Beckett waited until the trailing gunman was almost level with his hiding position before pushing off the slope toward him. His right shoulder hit the gunman in the chest, knocking him to the ground. The force of the blow along with Beckett's weight against him as they landed, knocked the gunman out cold. Beckett quickly stood up and mounted the gunman's horse.

Instead of heading for the lake, Mordecai broke into a gallop following the trail north, the wagon trying to keep up behind him.

Beckett chased after, finally pulling up alongside the driver. Reaching over, he grabbed the man by his belt and yanked him from his seat. The driver fell to the ground and rolled away. As the man riding shotgun raised his weapon,

Beckett dove from his horse and tackled him. The shotgun discharged harmlessly, startling the horses. Beckett struggled with the man briefly before slamming his head into the floor of the wagon then reined in the horse team. Expecting to see Mordecai charging back, he was surprised to find he was nowhere in sight.

Dumping the unconscious body of the shotgun guard over the side, he turned the wagon, driving it across the river then toward the abandoned mine.

ELI WAS SUPERVISING the burial of the dead miners when he heard the explosions. He was still deciding whether to ride down the trail when he saw Cincinnati. The deputy was disheveled with dirt all over his shirt.

"What the hell happened?" Eli yelled

"Beckett." Cincinnati's jaw was set and his eyes were narrow and cold as he stared ahead.

"The mountain man?"

"Get your men, we're going after him."

"Where's Mordecai?"

"I said get your men!"

Eli mounted his horse, calling for Clay and Jacoby to do the same. The three men followed Cincinnati down the road to the east, the road that led to Frank Gibson's cabin.

TWENTY-THREE

BECKETT LEANED against his sorrel to catch his breath. His pants were now completely dry but covered with dirt. After wiping dust from his hands and shirt, he reached into his saddlebag and retrieved his ball of clean rags and a small leather purse. From his teardrop-shaped bag he removed a fresh bottle of whiskey and the jar of lamp oil Jasper Baines had given him.

Sitting on the ground against a tree, he unbuttoned his shirt and pulled it down off his left shoulder. The bullet wound streamed blood. He unscrewed the lid from the jar of oil and dipped the tip of his Bowie into it. With one of the matches in his pocket, he lit the oil, holding the knife at arm's length to avoid the resulting fireball. It quickly burned out leaving the Bowie smoking.

He unhooked the hatchet from his belt. Clinching his teeth on the hatchet handle, he inserted the tip of the large knife into the wound. Pain was immediate. The smell of searing flesh soon followed. He dug into the wound until he felt hard metal. Thanks to grazing the bark off a tree before hitting him, the bullet wasn't very deep and had failed to hit his shoulder blade. Placing the knife tip underneath the metal, he pried the lead ball out, grunting and stifling a scream as he did so. When the metal reached the surface of the hole, he picked it out with the thumb and index finger of his right hand then tossed it aside. The hatchet fell from his mouth as a wave of relief swept over him.

After resting for a minute, he popped the cork on the whiskey bottle, took a good swig then poured a generous amount over the gaping hole, flinching as the liquid touched the wound. He let the pain dissipate awhile before opening the small leather purse and taking out a needle and thread.

He looked at the sorrel which was nosing around the pine needles covering the ground, looking for something to graze. "What color this time, black, red, green or blue?"

The horse only snorted, continuing his search.

"Black? Sure, seems like an appropriate color."

After threading the needle, he dipped both thread and needle into the bottle of whiskey. The residual pain from digging out the bullet masked tiny needle pricks as he sewed up the wound. Six stitches later, he doused the closed hole with more whiskey. Finally, he bandaged the shoulder with the clean rags from his saddlebag and buttoned his shirt.

He tried to pull himself up but his strength was gone. He fell back to the ground. As his eyes closed, he thought of Abby.

TWENTY-FOUR

ABBY LOOKED UP at the rolling grey clouds that had moved in since she'd begun stacking wood behind the cabin and wondered if it would rain. It wasn't dark enough yet in any direction to expect any moisture, but at this time of year, clouds meant there was a possibility. Even a sprinkle would be welcome relief for her small garden beside the cabin.

Her double action Colts were back on her hips. Earlier she'd taken them out to shoot the colorful heads off of wildflowers.

As the clouds thickened, she walked toward the front of the cabin and looked west to see if the chance of rain was improving. That's when four men rode out of the trees.

FRANK WAS STANDING on the front porch with his Henry rifle when he saw the men.

"Stay back, Abigail. Don't let 'em see you." He raised the Henry as the riders approached. "I'll take care of this."

His daughter hesitated before edging back behind the cabin.

The four men who had threatened them yesterday came to a stop, forming a half circle in front of the porch. The mutt Abigail called Baxter barked at them from behind the barn.

"I told you boys to stay off my land." Frank waved the end of his Henry in the direction of the trail to the west.

"Mr. Gibson, we have come for Beckett. Tell us where he is and we will leave you be."

The leader, Deputy Cincinnati as he recalled, was more curt this time, his eyes harder. His appearance was also changed. His attire was no longer pristine, but covered with dirt. There were even smudges on his face.

"He ain't here. Haven't seen him since he left this morning."

Cincinnati turned toward the man called Eli. "Check the stable."

Eli and the other two riders dismounted and pulled their weapons. As they headed for the stable, Cincinnati lowered himself from his horse and tied it to the railing on the porch.

"Come any closer and I'll blow your head off." Frank cocked the Henry.

"Now, Mr. Gibson. We don't need to resort to those measures do we?" Cincinnati's manner was more like before, calmer with an air of superiority. "All I have for you are a few questions."

"Bullshit." Frank dipped the end of the Henry at Cincinnati's side. "The only thing you got for me comes from the barrel of that gun on your hip."

Cincinnati looked down at his ivory-handled Colt. "I can assure you I have no intention of using my weapon. To prove it, I will drop my gun belt. Will you allow me to do so?"

"I don't give a shit what you do so long as you leave my property."

Cincinnati slowly moved his left hand to his thigh and pulled the knot loose that held his holster to his leg. As he bent over, the jewel around his neck sparkled. He then unlatched his belt buckle.

"See, Mr. Gibson. I am disarming myself. Might I ask you to do the same."

"Not a chance."

"Well, that doesn't seem quite fair." Cincinnati dropped the gun belt from his hips. As it fell, he caught the Colt with his right hand and fired, blowing a hole in Frank's chest, splattering blood on the door behind him. Cincinnati fanned two more shots into his abdomen before Frank hit the ground.

"I do not appreciate it when men draw their guns on me when I'm trying to be civil." Cincinnati picked up his gun belt and cinched it around his waist.

"DADDY, NO!" ABBY SCREAMED, running onto the porch. She slid on her knees beside him, cradling his convulsing body while supporting his head with the palm of her hand. Her father's eyes were wide. His lips formed words but made no sound as blood filled his mouth.

"It's gonna be okay, Daddy." She opened his shirt, tears pouring down her cheeks. "You're gonna be okay." Blood pulsated in warm streams from his wounds, making her fingers slip on the buttons. She gave up struggling with them and tore open his shirt.

His pale, wrinkled chest looked almost blue contrasted with the bright red that flowed out of it. The chest wound bubbled as he struggled for air.

She balled up the fabric of her dress skirt, pressing it on the wounds in a vain attempt to stop the bleeding. Looking into his eyes, she saw the muscles in his face relaxing. His gaze went through her as his body went limp. "Daddy?"

She pulled his face against her chest and held him as she cried. The tears came uncontrollably until she heard the familiar clink of fresh shells entering a revolver behind her. Tears of sadness we're replaced by tears of rage as she stood up and faced Cincinnati.

"That Beckett ain't here," Eli said, returning from the stable with his men. His eyes moved to Abby. "Well, lookie what we have here. You didn't shoot her did you?"

"No, Eli, I did not." Cincinnati placed the final bullet in his gun, snapped the cylinder into place, then slid it into his holster. "I was hoping to avoid any further bloodshed."

Abby looked down at the blood dripping from her hands and wiped them on her soiled, blue gingham dress skirt. Facing Cincinnati, she stepped down from the porch, her hands hovering over her pearl-handled Colts.

"Now, young lady, you aren't actually thinking about taking on a man like me with those guns are you?" Cincinnati's voice was cool and calm.

"She can take me on with 'em." Eli laughed and the other two men joined him.

"Just because you have a couple of revolvers doesn't mean you can kill me." Cincinnati smiled. "I'm faster than any man alive."

She took another step closer. "I ain't no man."

Abigail Gibson drew her guns.

TWENTY-FIVE

BECKETT WOKE to the sound of his horse neighing above him. He looked up at the clouds through pine branches, wondering where he was. He'd just been talking to Abby. Now she was gone.

His shoulder burned as he sat up, bringing everything back. He'd passed out from the pain of his gunshot wound and dreamed of a life with Abby, a life away from mines and explosions and gunfighters.

He checked the bandage on the wound and was satisfied it had not bled through. He'd done an excellent job patching himself up.

He couldn't tell how long he'd been out since the thick clouds blocked the sun. He was sure of one thing - Cincinnati and his men were looking for him.

He quickly packed up and mounted his sorrel. His boot heels jabbed the animal's ribs and they took off toward the place where he'd crossed the Coeur d'Alene before. After fording the river and reaching the trail at the base of the large hill, he heard hoof falls coming from the north. Riding into the trees, he jumped off his horse and pulled it to the ground on its side behind a strand of bushes. He knelt behind his sorrel as the animal tried to raise its head.

"Keep down," he whispered into the horses ear, caressing its neck.

Mordecai and four other men rode down the trail, stopping at the point in the river where Beckett had crossed.

"Reed. Holton. Cross the river and see if he took the route to the lake." Mordecai pointed west. "You other two come with me."

As Reed and Holton took off across the river, he said to the other two men, "Get your guns out. There had to be at least ten men who ambushed us. If any of them are here picking through the remains we'll get 'em."

Mordecai rode toward the mine, the men close behind.

Beckett remained behind his sorrel until the sound of their galloping disappeared in the distance. Pulling his horse up and mounting it, he turned east, riding as hard and as fast as he could through the trees to Frank and Abby's place.

TWENTY-SIX

AS ABIGAIL PULLED HER GUNS, she felt a sting in
her right arm just below her shoulder, then another in her
left. The impact of being hit altered her aim as she fired her
twin Colts. Her left-hand shot hit the ground a yard from
Cincinnati's right foot. The one from the right wounded
one of Eli's men in the calf.

She glared at Cincinnati, his gun out and smoking, his
left hand resting on the hammer. The man she'd acciden-
tally hit grabbed his wound, hopped on one leg and hollered.

The growing burn in her arms made her drop her guns.
Her hands reflexively crossed her chest to the pain. When
she took them away, they were covered in blood. This time
it wasn't her father's. Looking down, she saw two open
wounds through her torn dress, just below the shoulder of
each arm.

"Maybe I should revise that statement." Cincinnati
dropped two empty shells from his Colt. "I'm faster than
any man ..." He placed two new bullets in the chamber,
closed it and holstered the gun. His mouth widened into a

self-assured smile. "… or woman alive. You're lucky I decided just to graze you."

Cincinnati eliminated the distance between them in two quick steps, kicked her revolvers away in the dust and grabbed her by the hair. Baxter rounded the corner and barked at him.

Pulling her head back he hissed, "You listen. Now that Frank Gibson is gone, Sheriff Cain is the rightful owner of this property. Do you have a problem with that?"

Abigail didn't reply.

Cincinnati pulled her head back farther.

The "No" that came out of her mouth was more a squeak.

"Excellent." He let go of her hair and fluffed it around her shoulders, pushing a strand from her face with the back of his hand and gently placing it behind her ear. His hand slowly followed her cheekbone to her lips. He moved his thin mouth closer. "Then I guess you'd better get off our land."

He kept his eyes on her face as he backed away. Baxter continued barking from the side of the house. Cincinnati pulled his gun, casually cocked the hammer with his thumb, pointed it at the mutt and pulled the trigger. The explosion was followed by a yip, a squeal then silence. Cincinnati mounted his horse.

As Abigail looked at the other men, Eli was already heading toward her, the man she hadn't shot, close behind. Before she could react, Eli grabbed her arms, causing her to screech from the pain of her wounds. Though she struggled against him, Eli pulled her across the dirt toward the stable. When she fell to her knees, the other man lifted her legs and helped carry her through the open door.

Once inside, Eli forced her to the ground, rolling her on her back. Abigail managed to free her right arm and lashed out at his face. Eli cried out as her nails created three long gashes on his cheek.

Eli slammed her back down, straddling her as he reached back and punched her in the eye. Her head hit the ground with enough force that her vision went blurry. While she recovered her senses, the other man grabbed her hands, pulled her arms straight above her head then crushed her fingers into the bare stable ground with his knees. The man she'd shot hobbled in the open doorway, an eager expression on his face, as Eli tore open her dress revealing her thin lace chemise. He leered at her body as he reached to undo his belt.

He stopped at the sound of the gunshot and the puff of dust and hay that exploded an inch outside his right knee.

"That's enough, Deputy." Cincinnati stood in the doorway, his gun drawn and smoking again, his voice all business. "We have work to do."

Eli pounded the ground and said through clenched teeth, "Goddamn it! I ain't done here."

"Yes you are. Lets go, Eli." Cincinnati walked over beside him, his ivory-handled Colt menacingly close to Eli's face. "Now!"

Eli paused, looking at Abigail. Grunting, he got up off her and pushed the man who'd been holding her hands, toppling him into the hay. Eli walked to the door and punched the wall of the stable over and over until his knuckles left a bloody smear on the wood. He turned to the doorway and punched the hobbling man in the stomach. The man bent over, trying to catch his breath.

"If you are done with your tantrum, would you please get back on your horse?" Cincinnati reloaded and holstered his Colt.

As Abigail slowly sat up, the man who had been holding her hands stood and stumbled out of the stable. The man she'd shot limped out to his horse, holding his stomach. All three men mounted and rode off, leaving Cincinnati alone with her.

"Now, I'm a sympathetic man. I'm not just going to throw you out into the cold. I'm going to give you until sunrise to leave the premises. Does that sound fair?" He didn't wait for an answer. "Good."

As he mounted his horse, he added, "Oh, and I took the liberty of eliminating your pest problem."

Reaching behind his saddle, he tossed a long, furry object that landed in her lap. She looked down at a bloody, mottled grey tail with a white tip.

TWENTY-SEVEN

HIS SORREL'S BREATHING became strained as Beckett urged the animal to maintain a gallop down the dirt road. Despite the age of the horse, it was doing well keeping a steady pace. The rhythm of hooves on dirt and rock matched his heartbeat as wind whistled under the brim of his hat past his ears.

In the distance, he heard a gunshot coming from the direction of Frank's place. Then another. And another. He kicked the horse to push it even harder.

Clearing the trees and entering the valley from the west, he could see Frank's cabin up ahead, a lone figure standing out front. As he drew closer, he saw it was Abby with her two Colts in her hands. She fired four more shots into a pail in the yard as he reined his horse to a halt and slid out of the saddle.

"Abby," Beckett said, relief in his voice. "You're okay."

She didn't acknowledge his presence. Instead, she fired five more lightning quick shots tearing the wooden pail to pieces until the hammers of her Colts continued clicking against their empty chambers. Holstering her guns, she fell to her knees.

"Abby?" Becket rushed to her side.

"They killed him."

"They killed who?"

"My father. They killed him."

Beckett took a step backward as though he'd been slugged. He looked at the cabin and saw blood splattered on the door and pooling on the porch.

"Cincinnati?" Beckett said, knowing the answer.

"Shot him three times."

"I should have been here," he said to himself as much as to her.

"I wasn't afraid. I stepped up to him. I didn't care if he killed me. I was fast." She looked up at Beckett. "He was faster."

Fury was etched on her face, but her eyes were glossy, registering her pain. For the first time he noticed her dress was covered in blood and was unbuttoned down the front. There were two open wounds on her arms below her shoulders. She dropped her eyes from Beckett, returning her gaze to the ground. "I moved him off the porch. Couldn't get him any farther."

At the side of the house, Beckett saw a body slumped in the dirt. He moved toward it.

"Was gonna put him in the ground back by the big pine." Her voice indicated tears were moments away.

* * *

BECKETT TOSSED one last shovel full of dirt over the grave as the sun dropped behind the trees. He leaned on the shovel, looking at the mound of dirt. The large pine in the middle of the clearing loomed above him, throwing a long shadow across the fresh grave.

"I'm sorry, Frank. I'm sorry I let you down." He dropped to his knees. "You meant more to me than …"

He couldn't continue. He stood up and looked back towards the house. Abby was sitting on the porch steps. He planted the shovel in the ground and made his way toward her. As he got closer, he could see her reloading her Colts. He stopped at the base of the stairs, paused then took a seat next to her. They shared a moment of quiet, looking toward the trees.

"I did everything you said. I didn't back down, I came right at him."

"Some men ain't worth fightin'. Nothin' good can come of it."

"I thought I could protect us."

"Abby, I—"

"Abigail," she interrupted. "My father called me Abigail."

He studied her face. "Abigail, I should have been here."

"Should you have?" She looked at him, raising her voice. "What could you have done … with that knife? My father would have had a better chance takin' him out with his Henry. Don't care how intimidating you are. There's nothin' stoppin' a man like that."

Her eyes gave a hint of regret before she turned away.

"I was weak. I let them win."

"You tried. Nothin' much more you could do."

"No, I gave up. When I pulled my guns and he'd already shot me it was like I was a little girl again. I was scared. I let them ..." She glanced down at her open dress.

"You let them, what?"

"I let them win."

"What did they do?" Beckett said, hoping what he was thinking wasn't true.

"It ain't like that." She looked back at him. Her expression was softer, reminding him of the Abby he'd talk to on the porch in the starlight. "That Eli tried. He and the other fella - the one I didn't shoot - had me in the stable. I fought them but not hard enough. I should've fought harder but I was scared. They would've taken me if it weren't for Cincinnati callin' them off."

She put her hand on Beckett's. The warmth of her touch made him realize he'd clenched his hand into a fist so hard he'd lost feeling in it.

"It's over. I'm leavin'. Ain't got nothin' here. Don't even got Baxter no more." She took her hand away, pulled the mutt's tail from behind her gun belt and held it in her hands. "People like us ain't got no place here. We ain't like them, Beckett. We ain't killers."

Beckett looked down at the severed tail. The base was coated in dried blood. The tip was still bright white. He turned toward the orange glow of the lowering sun shining through the trees, feeling his pulse pound in his ears.

"You're right. You ain't like them. You ain't no killer."

He stood up and walked toward the stable where his horse was tied.

She stood to follow him. "Where are you goin'?"

"I'm goin' to end this."

TWENTY-EIGHT

VICTOR CLAY SAT on a log poking the fire with a long stick. At one point the flames had been intense. But now the fire just bellowed smoke toward the river despite there being plenty of wood. He jabbed the end of the stick into the heart of the pile, clearing a space for air to flow. A few moments later, thick flames were taking over again. He placed the stick against the log next to his '66 Winchester.

"I can't see shit with that lame excuse for a fire." Luther Jacoby sat on the ground across the fire from Clay, peeling a dirty bandage from his right calf. The sun had been down for an hour and the only light was their fire.

"Next time, you build one." Clay said, rolling a cigarette.

"How's it look?" Jacoby held his leg up. His pants were rolled to the knee, revealing wounds on either side of his calf that were black and shiny with dried blood.

"Looks like you got shot." Clay sealed the cigarette with his tongue and placed it in the corner of his mouth. He put the end of the stick he'd used before into the fire.

"No shit. Stupid bitch. Wish Cincinnati would've let us have a poke at her.'"

Clay pulled the stick from the fire and lit his cigarette with its flaming end. "Don't know if there'd been much worth pokin' once Eli was done with her."

"You seen what he does to the girls down at Rick's?" Jacoby dropped his leg into the dirt. "Saw him beat on a whore so bad her nose was sideways."

"Yup."

Jacoby poked at his wound with his dirty finger. He cringed at the touch and pulled it away. He held it to the light and looked at the dried mess he'd removed. "You think it looks infected?"

"What, your finger?"

"No. My leg, asshole."

"How should I know. I ain't no doctor."

"Think I should have the bartender at the saloon look at it?"

"Don't know if he'd care to see one of us on account of our boss killed his wife."

"Yeah, I guess." Jacoby carefully pulled his pant leg down over the wounds. "But don't doctors gotta see past shit like that? Ain't there some doctor code where they gotta take care of everybody?"

"Like I said, I ain't no doctor."

"Sure would've liked to have have a poke at that cherry down at Gibson's place. Might have been worth it even after Eli was done with her."

"Probably still there. You could pick some wildflowers and go and serenade her. Might just go for you willin'."

"Nah, girl like that wouldn't go for a guy like me," Jacoby said, not getting the joke. He thought about it for a moment. "You think singin' to her would work?"

"Goddamn, you are stupid."

"You're just jealous 'cause you ain't no good with women."

"I had her hands pinned. At least I was touchin' her while you were yankin' it in the doorway."

"I gotta take a piss." Jacoby pushed off of the dirt, groaning as he stood. He limped into the grove of birch trees, emitting an exaggerated grunt with every other step.

Clay slid onto the ground and leaned back against the log. He looked up at the sky. The clouds that had been there most of the day were starting to part, giving way to stars shining through the gaps. Nearby, he heard what sounded like a trout jumping in the river. The gentle sound of the running waters and the light breeze rustling the birch leaves above were lulling. He closed his eyes.

He was about to doze off when he heard a faint metallic clink behind him. He sat up and turned toward the sound. The light from the flickering fire danced on the white bark of the trees surrounding the clearing.

"Jacoby. That you?"

Jacoby hollered from the opposite direction. "Told you I was takin' a piss."

"Huh. Just thought I heard something." Clay turned back to the fire.

Noticing his cigarette had died out, he stuck the stick back into the fire. Before he could relight it from the burning stick, a muffled gasp came from Jacoby's direction. He stood up and reached for his Winchester. Even above the sound of the blazing fire, he could hear liquid pouring onto the ground.

Clay called into the darkness, "Jesus, how long does it take you to piss?" The dripping stopped. He waited. "Jacoby?"

Out of the shadows of the woods, a figure appeared, moving awkwardly toward the fire. Reaching the firelight, Clay saw it was Jacoby, his arms limp, his chest and pants covered in blood. As Jacoby came closer, the fire revealed the reason for the blood - his neck had been slit from ear to ear.

After his initial shock, Clay realized Jacoby wasn't moving under his own power. A large man behind Jacoby lifted up his dead body and threw it into the fire, sending sparks and glowing embers flying. Clay stepped back, tripping over the log he'd been sitting on. His back hit the ground hard enough to knock the wind out of him and loosen his grip on his Winchester. He quickly recovered and scrambled to his feet in search of his weapon.

As the large man walked over Jacoby's body and headed for him, Clay stumbled backwards toward the trees. He'd just reached the perimeter when the sound of metal on metal was instantly followed by screaming pain shooting up his leg. Looking down, he saw his left leg caught up to his shin in the jaws of a huge bear trap. With his hands he tried to pull open the metal teeth that had torn through the flesh of his lower calf and was biting into his shinbone. When the jaws wouldn't budge, he stomped down with the foot of his injured leg, trying to hit the trap's release trigger. The effort did nothing more than snap his shin, splitting the skin with shattered bone. His scream was short-lived, silenced by a huge fist hitting his temple.

BECKETT TIED a rope around Clay's wrists and threw it over a tree limb. As he hoisted him into the air, Clay awoke and immediately let out a scream.

"What the hell are you doing? My leg!" Agony was carved on Clay's face and his eyes showed panic.

Beckett pulled him higher until his body was stretched taut between his roped hands and his snared leg that was held by the bear trap anchored to a tree with a chain. Clay let out another scream as Beckett tied the rope off on a low limb.

"Where's Eli?" Beckett said.

"Let me down from here and I'll tell you whatever you want."

Beckett slammed his boot heel into the side of the trap. The sound of bone cracking was immediately followed by Clay's loudest cry yet.

"Where is Eli?"

"He's at the mine." Clay's words came out one at a time between strained breaths.

"Cincinnati there too?"

"Please let me down. My leg feels like it's about to come apart."

Beckett kicked the trap again, causing the jaws to close tighter. Clay's screams were now accompanied by a steady stream of tears.

"Is Cincinnati there too?"

"No. He went back to Temperance with Mordecai. We was supposed to meet 'em there in the mornin'."

Clay stopped struggling, apparently having passed out. Beckett slapped him across the face hard enough to bloody his nose. Clay's eyes shot open.

"What are their plans for the girl?"

Clay's words came out in a whisper. "Don't know. Cincinnati told her to get out by sunup. Eli stayed so he could go back and finish what he started with her."

"When?"

"Tonight."

Beckett unholstered his Bowie.

"Please. I didn't do nothin' to her."

"You did enough."

The blade slid into Clay's potbelly, cutting him from hip to hip then up to his sternum. As Clay blacked out, his insides spilled over the trail.

TWENTY-NINE

"I CAN'T BELIEVE what the fuck I'm hearing." Sheriff Cain stood behind his desk, leaning forward, his hands flat against the maple surface. Despite his irritation, he kept his voice calm. "First you come in here telling me that the mountain man blew up our shipment, sending it to the bottom of a ravine. Then you tell me you lost the first wagon because he had ten to fifteen men with him and you barely got out alive?"

Standing on the opposite side of the huge desk, Mordecai was unable to maintain eye contact with his father. He dropped his line of sight to his boots as beads of sweat appeared on his forehead. "Might have been less than ten men."

"And now after combing the area with all of our men you can't seem to find one hint of Beckett or these other supposed road agents. Is that what you're telling me?"

"Look, Pa, we checked all up and down the river and—"

"You're fucking done, Mordecai. You are fucking done!" Cain's voice boomed. Straining to control his anger, he added, "You've become more worthless than your worthless brother Eli."

"And you …" He turned toward Cincinnati who stood arm's length away from Mordecai. "You're the one I trusted. Did I not tell you you were in charge? Did I not tell you if this operation went to shit you would be held accountable?"

"Yes Sheriff Cain, you did." Cincinnati looked directly at the sheriff, but fidgeted with the hat he held in front of him.

"So where does that leave us? We have three tons of gold and ore sitting at the bottom of a ravine in two feet of water and another ton floating around in the woods somewhere with a magical, unarmed mountain man who seems to get the drop on every gun hand I own … oh and his ten magical friends, right Mordecai?" The grin on Cain's face belied the stern set of his jaw.

Mordecai glanced up, but quickly returned his gaze to his boots. "Said there might have been less than that."

"We did manage to acquire Frank Gibson's property outright." Cincinnati stopped moving the hat in his hands. "That will no longer be an issue."

"Oh, well thank the fucking lord for that, deputy. Now, when the spur to Wallace doesn't get built because you assholes managed to botch a simple wagon train job, we'll have a nice little cabin and a stable where we can braid each other's hair." Cain ground his teeth in growing frustration. "When do you expect the recovery of the gold in the ravine to be completed?"

"The men have pulled out a few of the unopened crates but the rest is slow going. Efforts stopped when night fell. I placed two men there with shotguns to prevent looting." Cincinnati's manner was reassuring. "All of the recovered gold has been secured at the mine. Eli is there overseeing it."

"And how goes the search for Beckett?"

"I have men stationed throughout the area. They will continue their search at sunup." Cincinnati gave a slight nod in Mordecai's direction. "Mordecai and I plan to form a posse of our remaining men and go after the mountain man."

Cain raised his eyebrows. "At sunup?"

"Yes."

Cain shook his head. "I have word that Zebadiah and his men will be here tomorrow. When he arrives I will hand the job over to him. I have full faith that he will be able to find Beckett and take care of the situation that you two have so completely fucked up!" Lowering his head, Cain took a deep breath then let it out slowly. He jabbed his right index finger onto the desk. "Guns."

Mordecai's brow furrowed in confusion. "What guns, Pa?"

"Your guns. Put your guns on my desk. Both of you."

The two men looked at each other. Cincinnati unholstered his Colt and flipped it in one fluid motion, placing it on the desk. Mordecai followed suit, dropping his revolver next to it.

Picking up Cincinnati's Colt, Cain opened the cylinder and dropped shells on to his desk one by one. The first bounced and rolled toward the deputies. The second hit and spun in place. "Cincinnati, how long have you worked for me?"

"Going on two years now I'd guess."

"And would you say you are familiar with how I like to run things? Could you imagine yourself in my shoes?"

"I suppose."

Another shell dropped from the cylinder, bounced then rolled off the desk to Cain's feet. "Well then, tell me, deputy, how would you handle a situation like this? One where two of your trusted employees failed you so completely that your business was in danger." Two more shells fell and hopped in opposite directions. "Would you reprimand them with a simple slap on the wrist?"

"If I were you?" Cincinnati placed his hat back on his head. "I'd have them killed."

Closing the cylinder, Cain laid the gun on his desk and slid it in Cincinnati's direction. "Yes, that does seem like the only option doesn't it?" He picked up Mordecai's gun, opened the cylinder and began dropping shells. "Mordecai, would you agree with Cincinnati's assessment?"

Mordecai's gaze was riveted on the falling bullets as worry crept into his eyes. "You can't kill us, Pa—"

"Do you agree with Cincinnati's assessment?" Cain snapped.

Mordecai again looked at his boots. "Yes."

Cain continued dropping shells. "Cincinnati, you're like a son to me, and Mordecai, you *are* my son, so I feel I should give you both one more chance. I'm going to let God himself decide your fate." After the fifth shell hit the maple and hopped off to the left, Cain closed the cylinder, placed the gun on the desk and slid it toward Mordecai. "I've left you each one round. Please pick up your weapons."

Cincinnati reached out and retrieved his Colt. Mordecai hesitated, first looking at Cincinnati then at his father, his eyes wide. His hand shook as he picked up his gun.

"Now, spin your cylinders and holster your guns."

Both men paused, looking at Cain.

"Go ahead. Spin them."

Cincinnati spun the cylinder and slid his Colt in his holster. Mordecai's hands were shaking so badly he fumbled his first effort, moving the cylinder only a couple of chambers. After his second try was successful, he slowly holstered the weapon, sweat streaming from his forehead.

"Okay boys, face each other and take a few steps back." Cain gestured with both hands as though separating the two men. Both complied though Mordecai's movement was slower. "Now, I'm going to count down from three and when I get to one you draw. Got it?"

Cincinnati gave a slight nod, his eyes locked on Mordecai while his hand hovered over his Colt.

Mordecai's whole body was trembling. "But, Pa, I ain't as fast as him."

"Three …"

Mordecai wiped his hands on his shirt as he looked into Cincinnati's eyes. He looked back to Cain and opened his mouth to talk.

"Two …"

Placing his hand on his gun, Mordecai tried to steady himself as a rivulet of sweat dropped off his bandaged nose.

"One."

Cain watched his son hurriedly pull his weapon. Before Mordecai could clear his holster, an empty click came from Cincinnati's gun. As a wave of relief washed over his face, Mordecai steadied his aim and pulled the trigger. No explosion followed, just another click as the hammer hit an empty chamber. For a moment, neither man moved. Then Mordecai dropped his gun and fell to his knees.

"Well, boys. God Almighty has decided to give you a second chance. If you don't catch Beckett and return my gold, I won't let God have any say in what I do to you from now on. Got that?"

"Yes sir." Cincinnati began reloading his Colt.

Mordecai stared at the floor in front of him. "Yes sir."

Cain slammed his fist onto the desk. "Now get the hell out of my office. And kill that son of a bitch mountain man."

THIRTY

ELI CAIN THREW his tattered saddlebag over the back of his horse and tied it down. He slid his '73 Winchester in its saddle holster and checked the two Colts at his hips. He raised his hand to his face, gingerly touching the three grooves the girl had made with her nails.

"Deputy Cain, what am I supposed to do if that mountain man comes around while you're gone? I'm just a foreman not a gunfighter," said a worn-out old miner.

"I don't give a shit what you do so long as he don't get into that building." Eli gestured toward the locked structure with two shotgun guards standing in front of it.

"Well, that's my point. Calvin and Albert ain't no gunmen neither. Don't know if either of 'em ever even used a shotgun before."

"It's the middle of the fucking night. If he was gonna try something it wouldn't be until morning anyway. I'll be back long before then to take over."

The horseshoe shaped mining camp was lit by multiple torches that lined the perimeter. Other than Eli, none of

Sheriff Cain's deputies remained. Only hired miners stood around their tents looking uneasy.

"I just don't think you leavin' is the best idea right now," the old miner said.

"I don't give a shit what you think, I got business to take care of." Eli mounted his horse. He yelled to the camp, "I'm leaving you in the hands of your foreman. If anything goes wrong while I'm gone, I'll kill each and every one of you starting with him."

Some shuffling of feet was the only reaction to the warning from the dirty and disheveled miners.

"We don't need any more fuck-ups like earlier today. Replacing each and every one of you would be no problem at all. Keep that in mind." Eli turned toward the road east. As he prepared to kick his horse to a gallop, something rough cinched around his neck, pulling him off of his ride. He hit the ground on his right shoulder. Dust plumed around him in the torchlight.

BECKETT DRAGGED ELI by the neck across the ground until he was looking down at him. As Eli's hands tried to relieve the pressure of the rope on his windpipe, Beckett kicked him in the mouth with his heel, knocking out both front teeth. Eli yelled, his hands moving from the rope to his bloody mouth.

While Eli moaned, squirming in pain, Beckett bent over and removed Eli's guns from their holsters then tossed them into an open rail car that was stopped at the end of the mine track.

Eli took his hands from his mouth. "My teef. You kicked out my teef."

"That was the point, yes."

"I'm gonna kill you." Eli spat blood into the dirt.

"I doubt that."

As Eli's hands clawed at the rope around his throat, Beckett hoisted him up hand by hand, his left shoulder burning with pain as he did so, then turned Eli so they were eye to eye. The tips of Eli's toes struggled to touch the ground.

Beckett surveyed the miners gathered in a loose semi-circle around them but nobody seemed eager to help Eli including the two with shotguns.

He returned his attention to Eli. "Where you off to?"

"None uf yer fucking business." Eli sprayed blood with each word.

Holding the rope up with his right hand, Beckett slammed the heel of his left into Eli's nose with enough force cartilage cracked. Eli cried out as blood spewed from his broken nose, streamed over his mouth and dripped off his chin.

Beckett let him swing awhile before speaking. "Where were you going?"

"Waf goin' to Gibfon's place." Eli's words were barely discernible through the flowing blood around and in his mouth.

"To do what exactly?"

Eli looked Beckett in the eye, anger showing through his pain. "I waf goin' to fuck yer girlfriend." He grinned then spit blood at Beckett.

Beckett wiped his face with his free hand. "Think she'd want your company do ya?"

"Don't gif a fuck what see want. Waf gonna gif it to her anyway."

Beckett unholstered his Bowie. "You were going to give her, what … your pecker? No need to ride all the way out there for that." Beckett placed the fourteen-inch knife blade up under Eli's crotch. "I can take it to her for you."

As he let go of the rope and Eli dropped onto the Bowie, Beckett yanked up cutting through fabric and soft flesh until the blade hit the pubic bone. Eli fell backward in a curled up ball, holding his bloodied manhood, screaming.

Beckett turned to the miners. "You fellas are just hired hands and I have nothin' against you. Cain's probably taken advantage of you as much as anybody. If you help me this will go much smoother. If not …" He ran his thumb and finger along the blade of his Bowie, cleaning off Eli's blood and flicking it to the dirt. He held up his knife into the torchlight. "Are we gonna to have any problems?"

No sound came from the miners though a couple shook their heads.

"Good. Now, first I'll need you to open that locked building."

During the next half hour, the miners transferred the remaining gold into three cars that sat at the terminus of the rail to the mine. When finished, Beckett instructed them to top off two of them with barrels of blasting powder while he lined the front car with sticks of dynamite. Finally, he selected four miners to help him push the two cars with the blasting powder up to the entrance until they began coasting down the slight slope into the mine.

Beckett walked over to Eli who was rocking back and forth on the ground with his hands between his legs, whimpering.

"Still hurt?"

Eli didn't respond, but just kept rocking.

"No worry. It will be over soon."

Beckett grabbed the rope and pulled Eli across the dirt. When he reached the first rail car, he lifted Eli into it and placed him in a sitting position on the bed of dynamite. After looping the rope around Eli's hands, he tied him to the handle of the car.

He walked over to his sorrel, removed the jar of lamp oil from his bag, then returned to Eli. "Sorry your death has to be so long and painful." He unscrewed the top of the oil jar. "'Course you earned it."

Beckett poured the oil over Eli's head and chest where it spilled onto his arms and legs. He reached into his pocket for his box of matches, lit one and tossed it into Eli's lap. Eli's agonized whining changed to an explosive scream as he went up in a ball of fire.

Beckett ducked his shoulder and pushed the final car toward the entrance, gaining momentum along the way until he reached the point where the slope took over. The car coasted into the mine, Eli's scream disappearing in the darkness with it.

Several seconds later a huge explosion rocked the hill, sending a few large rocks down into the camp, knocking a couple of torches to the ground and collapsing one of the miner's tents. Smoke and dust gushed from the mine until it was choked off by dirt and rock filling the entrance.

Beckett turned and looked at the miners around him. "This mine is closed."

THIRTY-ONE

THE SUN WAS just coming up, lighting the eastern sky behind the trees as Jasper Baines closed the front door of his shop and walked out onto the wood sidewalk. It would be awhile before its glow would warm things, though. His breath was visible in the crisp morning air.

He'd taken a couple steps when a voice behind him caused him to stop.

"Jasper, where are you going?" Lilly Bains peeked from behind the front door, still in her nightgown with her hair mussed from sleep.

"Told you I was goin' to that meetin'." Jasper kept his voice low while taking quick glances over each shoulder.

"I don't want you a part of that. They're only looking for trouble."

"I got to. I promised Samuel I would." He looked up at the second floor where his son's room was located. Two eyes watched him from behind the glass.

"Fine. Go, hear what they say but don't get involved."

"I won't, dear." Jasper continued down the sidewalk.

The front of Sherman Saloon was closed up and the curtains pulled. Jasper turned into the alley, avoiding the entrance. Looking in both directions, he slipped in the unlocked back door of the saloon.

The room was almost dark with only a few lamps and candles providing light. The glow from the rising sun outside came in faintly below the drapes covering the front windows. Doc Sherman stood behind the bar and Harvey Coleman sat on a stool across from him. Most of the men of the town filled chairs or lined the walls. Everyone turned and looked at Jasper as he entered the room.

"Jasper, good to see you" Doc said. "Have a seat if you can find one."

Jasper scanned the room as he walked along the far wall, selecting one of the poker tables in the corner to lean against. As he put his weight on the table, it rocked forward. He reflexively stood up. The base of the table slammed down onto the hollow wood floors, the sound reverberating across the quiet room. Jasper's cheeks went red. He apologized then stood with his hands in his pockets.

"We'd only just started so you didn't miss much, Jasper," Doc said. "Now, like I was saying, Harvey here heard at the mine that Cain has another son who is on his way to Temperance. Says this one's the worst of 'em all. If he plants more roots here with these new men our town is as good as gone. Hell, might as well just call it Cainstown."

"Why don't we just wait until that Beckett fella takes care of 'em? Said he had his own plan for Cain," said one

of the miners Jasper didn't recognize. "What if that in-
cludes runnin' him out of town?"

"We can't depend on maybes or what-ifs. For all we
know Beckett had a discussion with Cain, came to an
agreement then left town," Harvey said. "This is our town,
not his. We need to stand up to them."

"I think most of us agree with you, Harvey. That's why
we're here, right men?" The room grunted and nodded af-
firmatively. Doc continued, "So, the question is what are we
gonna do about it?"

For the next hour the men discussed their options from
signing a petition and getting government help to arming
up and storming Cain's office. None of the participants
seemed too happy with any of the ideas.

As his attention wavered, Jasper looked around the
room. Harvey Coleman had his large gun out of its holster
and was clicking the cylinder around examining the ammu-
nition. The black piano player sat on the bench in front of
the piano, digging at the bandages on his left hand with an
unbandaged finger. Just beyond the piano in the corner by
the back door was a small figure. Jasper squinted in the
dimness.

"Samuel!" He headed across the room, grabbing the
boy by the arm. "What are you doing here?"

"I wanted to see how you was gonna take down Cain
and his men."

"This ain't no place for a boy." He pulled Samuel out
the back door and placed him against the wall in the alley.
"Now, I want you to head straight home. I'll be back when
I'm done here."

Samuel looked at the ground and kicked the dirt.

"And I don't want you tellin' your mother about anythin' you heard. It would only upset her."

"I won't, Pa."

"Good." Jasper opened the back door to the saloon. "Now, head on home."

SAMUEL STOOD AGAINST the wall for a moment, the smell from the outhouse to his right making his stomach turn. He pinched his nose with his fingers and turned toward Main Street, dragging his feet in the dust. The sun was high enough now to bathe the dusty street in warm golden light.

THIRTY-TWO

SHERIFF CAIN STOOD on the landing behind his office smoking a cigarette. The smoke filling his lungs had a calming effect on him. The sun had just appeared above the trees and warmed his face as a pair of deer zig-zagged between pines sprinkled on the rise behind the bank. He closed his eyes for a moment, soaking up the sunlight. When he opened them, his eyes took a few seconds to adjust before finding the deer again.

At the moment he picked them out in the pines, the deer stopped, their ears pointing forward as they looked in his direction. He wondered why they'd just now noticed him when he felt a presence above. The wooden landing shook as someone dropped down from the roof behind him. Before he could react, a large hand tore his hat off and grasped his hair, pulling his head back. He felt cold steel placed below his Adam's apple.

"Mr. Beckett I presume." He kept his voice steady while being forced to look up at the sky.

"Is Mordecai the only one inside?"

"Deputy Mordecai is the only one inside, yes." Cain remained calm. "We have a few things we'd like to discuss with you if you have the time." As he swallowed, the knife cut into the skin just below the stubble.

"We're going to turn around slowly and you're going to open the door," the man with the knife said.

"Sure, be glad to."

SAMUEL WAS WALKING across Main Street in front of Sherman Saloon, looking at his feet while in deep thought, when he ran face first into a man's back.

"Gee, mister, I'm sorry …" He glanced up as the man turned around.

Looking down at him was Cincinnati, his small mouth stretched in a wide grin. When he bent over, Samuel came eye to eye with the polished ruby on Cincinnati's necktie. It was so big he could see his reflection in it.

"Well, if it isn't the mountain man's little friend." Cincinnati's grin slowly evaporated. "You really should try to be more careful when you cross the street. You never know who you could run into."

Samuel had never been this close to the deputy before. He wondered if, in fact, he was standing face-to-face with Duke Valentine, the vicious killer from his dime novels. His eyes were drawn to the leather band around Cincinnati's right arm. Was there a heart shaped brand under it? As much as he was afraid of the man in front of him, he was equally fascinated by him.

As Samuel's eyes tracked down to the gun at the deputy's side, Cincinnati slid his Colt from the holster. "Are you interested in guns?"

Samuel knew all about them from his books. This one was a .45 caliber Single Action Army Peacemaker with an ivory handle. The exact same gun Duke Valentine carried.

"Maybe I could show you how it works."

IT TOOK A FEW MOMENTS for Beckett's eyes to adjust to the dimness of Sheriff Cain's office. The two windows that faced south were small and didn't let in much light. The sun wasn't high enough yet to brighten the room through the two larger windows looking down on Williams Street.

Beckett pushed Cain ahead of him and into the room, holding his head back, the blade of his Bowie pressed against his Adams's apple.

Mordecai shot out of his chair when he saw them, his nose still taped from when Beckett had broken it.

"Drop the gun." Beckett nodded at Mordecai's revolver.

Mordecai paused then, keeping his eyes on Beckett, yelled toward the open windows behind him, "Beckett's up here."

"Shut your mouth and drop your gun or his head is coming off." Beckett increased the pressure on the blade, cutting into Cain's skin. Blood trickled down Cain's neck to his shirt collar.

Seeing the blood, Mordecai placed his hand on his gun.

"Slowly," Beckett said.

Mordecai removed his weapon and dropped it on the floor at his feet.

"Kick it away."

Mordecai complied.

"Now, have a seat."

As he sat, Mordecai looked toward the front windows as though they were the source of their salvation.

"Why don't you let me go so we can have a civilized conversation." Cain's voice was still calm, his body relaxed against Beckett.

"I think we're fine right here."

"There's no way out of this for you, Beckett. Even if you manage to kill us both, the second you walk out that door Cincinnati will fill you full of so many holes you'll whistle in the wind." Despite his precarious position, Cain managed a smile.

"Already killed one of your deputies today. Don't have any extra holes because of it."

Mordecai sat forward in his chair. "You killed Eli?"

"Couldn't have happened to a more deserving fella you ask me." Beckett felt Cain's body tense.

"What do you want?" Though still calm, Cain's voice was beginning to reflect the strain of his circumstance.

"I want you gone and I want Cincinnati dead."

"Well, that is not going to happen," Cain snapped.

"Then neither of you boys is leavin' this room alive. Already went through the trouble of shuttin' down your mine for you. All you got to do now is pack up and leave."

"What did you do to the mine?" For the first time, there was uncertainty in Cain's tone.

"Closed it for good. Sealed Eli's burnin' corpse inside with a ton of explosives. My ears are still ringin' from the blast."

A tremor ran through Cain's body as his teeth ground together.

"So what's the answer? Am I going to pull this knife through your neck so your head hangs off then gut your idiot son or are you going to pack up and leave?"

Cain remained quiet.

The silence was broken by Cincinnati's voice coming from the street. "Mr. Beckett, is that you up there? I hope the sheriff is showing you his usual hospitality?"

Beckett moved Cain toward the windows.

CINCINNATI GRABBED Samuel and pulled him close, lifting him slightly off the ground, Samuel's chin resting on Cincinnati's leather arm band. He struggled to get away until he felt the cold steel barrel of Cincinnati's Colt on his temple.

"I was just having an engaging conversation with your little friend here." Cincinnati raised his voice to the windows of the Sheriff's office.

"He's got a knife at Pa's throat," Mordecai yelled from inside the office.

"Well now, Mr. Beckett. I know we haven't gotten off on quite the right foot but is that really the best way to treat your new friends?"

"Let the boy go." Beckett looked down from the window, still holding his knife at the throat of Sheriff Cain.

"Only if you let the sheriff go first. That's how this works. That's what happens when I have the upper hand."

Men came out of the saloon onto the sidewalk. Samuel saw his father among them. When he'd realized what was happening his father cried, "Samuel, no!"

"What's it gonna be, Beckett?"

Beckett didn't answer.

Cincinnati cocked the hammer on his Colt. Samuel felt the metallic clicks reverberate through his skull. "Say goodbye to—"

He stopped when he heard Mordecai's voice. "I got him! I got Beckett!"

"Well now, that's more like it." Cincinnati gestured to one of his men on the street. Samuel remembered Mordecai calling him Reed.

As Reed came over, unholstering his gun as he approached, Cincinnati shoved Samuel at him. "Hold onto the boy until I give you the all clear."

Samuel watched as Cincinnati holstered his Colt and hurried toward the bank with purposeful strides.

THIRTY-THREE

WHEN BECKETT'S HEAD hit the floor, his vision went blurry. As his eyes cleared and his senses returned he remembered how it happened. After he'd let go of Cain, Mordecai jumped him and threw him to the ground. He'd then been lifted up by the shirt and pounded with a massive fist that bounced his head off the wooden floor. And now Cincinnati was coming up the stairs.

"Well, well, well." Cincinnati walked over and stood over Beckett. "How are we doing up here?"

"He killed Eli." Though there was a whine to Mordecai's voice, there was fury in his eyes as he took Beckett's Bowie knife and put it in his belt.

"And he destroyed the mine." Cain wiped blood from his neck. "I want him dead."

"Well, now, wait a minute Sheriff." Cincinnati held up his hand. "Shouldn't we try to find out what he did with the fourth wagon full of gold before we go ending his life?"

Mordecai pounded Beckett's head into the floor again. "Where's the wagon,"

"Mordecai, get off of him." Cincinnati's voice was relaxed. "We can't get answers out of him if his brain is jelly. Besides, won't it be more satisfying to make him suffer?" He smiled down at Beckett. "Place him in the chair, would you?"

Mordecai grunted as he picked Beckett off the floor and dropped him into a chair.

Cincinnati looked at Cain. "Sheriff, do you mind if I conduct the interrogation?"

Cain nodded. "That's what I hired you for. Besides, he came here looking for you. He wanted you dead."

Cincinnati turned toward Beckett. "Me? You wanted me dead?" His smile broadened. "What on earth for?"

Beckett's head was pounding. He shook it to clear the cobwebs. "You killed Frank Gibson."

"Well, that is true. I did kill Frank Gibson. Of course, I had no choice. He did have a Henry rifle on me."

Reaching over, Cincinnati pulled the Bowie out of Mordecai's belt then leaned over Beckett.

"How were you going to kill me?" Cincinnati brandished the knife blade a few inches from Beckett's face. "Were you going to use this here Bowie knife? Maybe do something like this?"

Cincinnati shoved the knife point into Beckett's wounded left shoulder, striking bone. A yell escaped between Beckett's teeth as he grabbed for the knife. Cincinnati pulled it away, holding it teasingly out of reach.

"I'm sorry. It looks like you were already wounded there. Is that a gunshot? Who could have done that? Oh, that's right, I shot you there ... right after you blew up six of our men and ran off with one of our wagons." Cincinnati leaned in closer. "Where did you take our wagon, Mr. Beckett?"

DOC STOOD on the corner in front of his saloon with his ten-gauge shotgun in his hand. Harvey and Nat stood next to him. The rest of the town had come out onto the street and were watching Reed as he held a gun to Samuel's head. Jasper Baines was a few buildings down holding his wife who was crying and calling out to her son.

"We can't let them do this," Harvey said. "We can take him."

"If we go at Reed, he'll put a bullet in the boy's head," Doc cautioned. "That's not something I can fix."

"NO ANSWER? Did you forget, by chance where you took the wagon?" Cincinnati stood back, looking at the large knife he held. "I hear that lead poisoning can make you forget things. Did you not pull that bullet out before you stitched yourself up? Why don't we make sure? Mordecai, would you hold our guest's hands please?'

Mordecai moved over to Beckett, leaned down and clamped his two giant hands on Beckett's forearms near the wrists, forcing them back behind the chair. Beckett cringed as pain shot through his shoulder.

Cincinnati stepped up to Beckett and gently inserted the tip of the Bowie into the open wound then twisted it. Beckett tried to pull away but was unable to overcome Mordecai's strength. As the knife dug in deeper, Beckett heard it scraping bone. He concentrated on not yelling.

"Still no answer? Well, how about we take a break and move on to something a little bit easier?" Cincinnati removed the knife. "We would like to acquire your gold claim. Before I kill you I'd like to know where you keep the deed. Finding it will save on paperwork down the road."

Beckett slumped in the chair. He kept his breathing steady, trying to control the pain.

Still holding his arms behind him, Mordecai nodded his head at Beckett's backside. "He's got something in his pocket."

Beckett tensed knowing exactly what he'd found.

Cincinnati reached around and removed the folded up envelope from Beckett's back pocket. "Well, this might just have saved us a little trouble." Cincinnati placed the Bowie on Cain's desk and opened the envelope. Pulling out one of the papers he read, "'Dearest Daniel, I dreamed about that night again …'"

Beckett struggled against Mordecai with all his strength, forgetting the intense pain it caused. He had one hand almost free before Mordecai closed his hands in a viselike grip and tugged his arms back.

Cincinnati continued, " … I will never forget that night in Durango ten years ago.' Durango?" He looked up from the paper. "I spent some time in Durango going on … well, ten years ago. It's amazing we didn't run into each other while we were there. Who is this Daniel?" Cincinnati laughed. "He isn't your lover is he?"

Beckett propelled himself forward using his legs, momentarily catching Mordecai off balance before the large deputy pulled him back to the chair.

"Oh, does this letter mean something to you?" Cincinnati flipped through the envelope. "Do all these letters mean something to you?"

Beckett remained quiet, gritting his teeth.

Cincinnati walked behind Cain's desk, pulled out one of the drawers and reached inside. As he turned his back to him, Beckett heard a familiar sound then the smell of burning sulfur. Cincinnati turned and walked back around the desk, holding the envelope of letters out in front of him, flames well on their way to engulfing them.

"No!" Beckett was unable to hide the grief in his voice.

Mordecai pulled harder on his arms.

"Well, I hope they weren't too important." Cincinnati dropped the burning papers on the floor, watching until they were nothing more than black ash dancing in the breeze coming from the window. Turning back to Beckett, he said, "Now, let's talk about that wagon."

WHAT IF one of us sneaks up behind him?" Harvey said.

"There ain't enough room to maneuver. Our backs are pretty much up against the wall. We can't risk the boy's life." Doc answered.

Their discussion was interrupted by several loud thumps coming from the bank, sounding as if someone had fallen down the stairs.

A moment later Beckett stumbled out of the bank door, kneeled on the porch then rolled down the two steps to the street, his shirt sleeve catching a nail on the way.

Cincinnati came out behind him followed by Mordecai and Sheriff Cain. Reaching Beckett first, Cincinnati kicked him in the face.

Beckett pulled his shirt free and tried to stand but was unable to for long, faltering a few steps into the street before Cincinnati kicked him in the back, pushing him face first in the dirt.

Beckett kept going, clawing the ground, pulling his broken body away from the bank.

THIRTY-FOUR

SAMUEL STRUGGLED against Reed as he watched Beckett crawl down the center of Williams Street directly toward them. As Beckett neared the middle of the intersection where Williams formed a "T" with Main, he raised himself to his knees.

Reed backed away a couple yards further up Williams, dragging Samuel with him. Instead of continuing toward them, Beckett managed to stand and turned up Main. He was hunched over and his stride was unsteady as he passed Sherman Saloon on his left and Main Street Hotel on his right. Then he collapsed to his knees before falling face-first into the dirt.

While Beckett had crawled down Williams, Cincinnati slowly kept pace, paralleling the mountain man's progress, walking down the wooden sidewalk from the bank to the jail. When Beckett turned down Main, Cincinnati stepped into the middle of Williams where Samuel and Reed first stood. Sheriff Cain joined Cincinnati, standing a few steps from his left. Mordecai followed suit, another few steps to the left of his father.

Samuel's attention was then drawn to the saloon where Harvey Coleman had just come into the street. Behind him on the sidewalk, Doc Sherman held his ten-gauge shotgun with Nat the piano player next to him.

Beckett again pulled himself to his knees, his back to Cincinnati.

"Are you having a little trouble standing up there, Mr. Beckett?" The thumb of Cincinnati's right hand was looped inside his belt buckle. He rested his left on the hilt of Beckett's Bowie knife which he'd slid behind his belt.

Beckett struggled to stand before turning toward Cincinnati.

Harvey Coleman took another step into the street.

"Well it looks as if we have ourselves an old fashioned standoff, now don't we," Cincinnati said. "The only problem is, not all of us are armed. It seems I have your only weapon, Mr. Beckett."

Cincinnati pulled the Bowie from his belt and threw it at Beckett. It slid in the dirt before landing two feet short of his boots. "Now, even though I've given you back your only weapon, this situation still doesn't seem quite fair. You can't have a gunfight if not everyone has a gun."

Cincinnati looked directly at Harvey who was now nearly to the middle of Main. "Sir, would you mind loaning your revolver to Mr. Beckett there? It seems he forgot to bring a gun."

Harvey stopped, his hand hovering over the gun at his side. Samuel thought for sure he was going to draw. Instead he turned and walked toward Beckett.

"Now, if you would please undo his knife belt and place your gun belt on him instead, I'm sure he would greatly appreciate it." Cincinnati wore a confident smile, his left hand hanging loose at his side, his right still perched on his belt buckle.

Harvey looked back at Doc then approached Beckett. He unbuckled Beckett's belt and dropped it to the ground. He then removed his own gun belt, placing it around Beckett's hips. As he cinched the buckle Samuel saw Harvey's mouth form the words "I'm sorry, Beckett."

As Harvey backed away to join the rest of the crowd that had gathered on the sidewalk, Cincinnati said to him, "Well now, that's some gun you've got there. Is that a Walker Colt?" He directed his next comment to Beckett, "That's a pretty powerful sidearm. A little too big to be useful in a quick draw but at least you have something."

Tears welled up in Samuel's eyes as he looked at Beckett standing alone in the middle of Main Street facing Cincinnati. Beckett's hat was gone. His face was battered, his left eye swollen shut. Blood flowed from his nose and mouth. His left shoulder bled heavily from a gaping wound that showed beneath his torn shirt. His right sleeve was nearly detached at the shoulder, baring pale skin which gleamed in the sunlight. Harvey's Walker Colt rode low on his right hip and his Bowie lay in the dirt in front of him.

Cincinnati's voice dried up Samuel's tears. "Well, here we are. Now, I'm not one for drawing first and you don't appear to have a gun raised at me. The only civilized thing to do now would be to have a countdown" Cincinnati turned to Samuel. "Boy, would you mind counting down from five?"

Turning back to Beckett, he said, "We draw at one, okay?"

Beckett didn't say anything. He stood hunched over with his eyes on the ground.

"Any time, boy." Cincinnati stood relaxed.

Samuel remained quiet until Reed jabbed his knee into his back. He squeaked out, "Five …"

He heard nervous low voices from the crowd gathered on the sidewalks, punctuated by the sound of his mother crying.

"Four …"

In front of the saloon, Doc Sherman raised his shotgun. The men around him who had hand guns reached for them. Doc nodded across the street to Seamus McCready who raised his rifle in front of the hotel.

"Three …"

A thin smile crossed Cincinnati's face as he stared down his opponent.

"Two …"

Beckett still stood with his shoulders slumped, his head facing the ground. His eyes may have been on his Bowie, but Samuel couldn't tell for sure. Both hands were limp at his side. The sun, now directly over the jail, bathed his injured face in light.

"One."

As Samuel said the word he looked at Cincinnati who drew his Colt and pulled the trigger so fast it was a blurred flash. Dust puffed up two feet in front of the deputy as the bullet hit the ground. Samuel looked back at Cincinnati to see the huge ruby on his tie had shattered. Blood was coming from his chest. Cincinnati dropped his gun and fell backwards into the street.

Cain and his men froze in shock.

Samuel turned toward Beckett. He was no longer slouched over. His feet were spread and his body alert. Harvey's Walker Colt was smoking in his hand.

In the blink of an eye, Beckett fanned three more shots.

The first hit Mordecai in the chest.

The second took off the top of Sheriff Cain's head.

The third sprayed Samuel in a mist of blood as a bullet entered Reed's right eye. Samuel broke away just before Reed's body tumbled to the dirt at his feet.

When he looked back over at Mordecai, he noticed that the deputy, though hit, was still standing, immobile like a giant statue in the street. Beckett fired two more lightning quick shots. The bullets tore into Mordecai's chest near his previous wound. The big man teetered then fell hard to the ground.

Despite the number of people lining the streets, Temperance was silent. The air was thick with black powder smoke.

Beckett threw the empty revolver down where it hit with a solid thud, kicking up dust. As he unhooked and dropped the gun belt from his hips, he limped over to Doc and gestured for his ten-gauge. Doc handed it over.

Hobbling over to Cincinnati, he straddled his body. He placed the shotgun under Cincinnati's chin and cocked one of the hammers.

Between choking breaths, Cincinnati's hand made grabbing motions, touching nothing but air. One grab inadvertently tore Beckett's right sleeve the rest of the way from his shoulder. It slid down his arm to his forearm.

Cincinnati's eyes were wide as he looked up into Beckett's. His voice gurgled, "I wanted to be you."

"No one should be like me." Beckett pulled the trigger. Cincinnati's head exploded in a cloud of blood, bone and brain.

Beckett limped over to Mordecai who was still thrashing on the ground, fighting for breath. As Doc and Nat joined him, Samuel ran over to get a better view, gazing at the gaping holes in Mordecai's chest. Beckett exchanged a glance with Nat and handed the ten-gauge shotgun to the black piano player, placing his hand on his shoulder. Nat nodded at Beckett.

As he passed Samuel on the way to the Sherman Saloon, Beckett pulled the sleeve that hung from his right forearm and threw it to the ground. On his right arm, just below his elbow was a brand in the shape of a heart.

THIRTY-FIVE

BECKETT ENTERED Sherman Saloon and walked around the bar. He reached up to the top shelf with a pained grunt and pulled down a bottle of rye whiskey. Grabbing a glass, he moved to the front of the bar and sat on a stool with his back to the door.

As he poured himself a glass, a second shotgun blast came from the street followed by gasps and screams. He downed the shot and poured another.

A few moments later, he watched in the mirror as Samuel quietly slipped into the saloon and walked silently to the bar, sitting two stools to Beckett's right. He was soon followed by Doc and what seemed like the rest of the town as they formed a semicircle a safe distance around Beckett.

"You're him," Samuel said. "You're Duke Valentine."

Beckett drank another shot of rye and refilled the glass. "Yes."

"Why do you go by Beckett?"

"'Cause that's my name. Beckett Valentine." Beckett drained the glass again. "Boys on the range used to call me Duke. Don't remember why."

"I can't believe you're Duke Valentine," Samuel shook his head. "Why did you kill that boy?"

"That boy was my son." Beckett refilled the glass and immediately downed it. "We rode into town, I dropped him off and told him to stay out of trouble. Then I went drinkin'. I knew I was the fastest gun alive and when I drank I liked to prove it. I eventually ended up in the same place my boy had decided to stay, although, at the time I didn't know it. I got into a gunfight and fired one too many shots. The last one went into Daniel's chest." He poured one last drink and finished it. "I was so drunk I didn't even realize what I'd done until the next morning. As soon as he was buried, I disappeared."

"But I looked up to you." Tears formed in the corners of Samuel's eyes.

"I ain't someone you should be lookin' up to. I ain't nothin' but a no good killer." Beckett stood and limped through the crowd of people that parted as he approached.

After going out the saloon doors, he stepped into the street. Nat stood with the smoking ten-gauge in his hands, still looking at Mordecai whose brains were scattered all over Williams Street.

The saloon crowd trickled out onto the sidewalk as Beckett picked up his belt and cinched it. He groaned as he bent to retrieve his Bowie then placed it in his holster.

With the town watching, Beckett Valentine walked down Main Street on his way out of Temperance.

EPILOGUE

BECKETT ENTERED the diamond-shaped clearing at its northern most point. He rode straight to the cabin and opened the door. It had been abandoned. He turned and looked toward the stable. The doors were open and the horses were gone.

He sat at the table in the corner and dropped his bag on the floor next to it. He removed his pen and inkwell and placed them in front of him. Pulling a blank sheet of paper from the cigar box, he began to write. Before he could scratch out a single word, he saw something out of the corner of his eye.

In the doorway stood a mottled grey mutt. It had a white front paw and was wagging the stump where its tail had been.

ACKNOWLEDGMENTS

I WOULD LIKE to thank my editor, Michael L. Johnson and my proofreader, L.M. Kildow for helping me look like I know what I'm doing and for getting me hooked on Westerns in the first place. I would also like to thank my friend and brilliant photographer, Mark Locke for all his hard work and support over the years. Finally, thanks to Isaac Kantor for giving me some great ideas while enjoying a couple of beers at the Moon Time alehouse in Coeur d'Alene.

Mark Locke Creative

MATT PRESCOTT, a native of Seattle, is a small business owner and musician who has worked in the music industry for nearly twenty years. He has spent every summer of his life visiting family in beautiful Coeur d'Alene, Idaho and truly has a love for the area. It is because of this love and his passion for westerns that *Temperance* came to be. Prescott now lives in Coeur d'Alene with his wife and daughter.

matt-prescott.com
facebook.com/MattPrescottAuthor
twitter.com/MPrescottAuthor

Made in the USA
Middletown, DE
10 August 2015